The Bar at Twilight

ALSO BY FREDERIC TUTEN

My Young Life: A Memoir

Self Portraits: Fictions

The Green Hour

Van Gogh's Bad Café

Tintin in the New World

Tallien: A Brief Romance

The Adventures of Mao on the Long March

The Bar at Twilight

FREDERIC TUTEN

Bellevue Literary Press
New York

First published in the United States in 2022
by Bellevue Literary Press, New York

For information, contact:
Bellevue Literary Press
90 Broad Street
Suite 2100
New York, NY 10004
www.blpress.org

The painting on the front cover is *Encounter in the Mountains* by Frederic Tuten.

This is a work of fiction. Characters, organizations, events, and places (even those that are actual) are either products of the author's imagination or are used fictitiously.

Library of Congress Cataloging-in-Publication Data

Names: Tuten, Frederic, author.
Title: The bar at twilight / Frederic Tuten.
Description: First Edition. | New York : Bellevue Literary Press, 2022.
Identifiers: LCCN 2021033774 | ISBN 9781954276031 (paperback) |
ISBN 9781954276048 (ebook)
Subjects: LCGFT: Short stories.
Classification: LCC PS3570.U78 B37 2022 | DDC 813/.54--dc23
LC record available at https://lccn.loc.gov/2021033774

Bellevue Literary Press would like to thank all its generous donors—individuals and foundations—for their support.

This project is supported in part by an award from the National Endowment for the Arts.

This publication is made possible by the New York State Council on the Arts with the support of the Office of the Governor and the New York State Legislature.

Book design and composition by Mulberry Tree Press, Inc.

Bellevue Literary Press is committed to ecological stewardship in our book production practices, working to reduce our impact on the natural environment.

First Edition

10 9 8 7 6 5 4 3 2

paperback ISBN: 978-1-954276-03-1

ebook ISBN: 978-1-954276-04-8

For Iris Smyles

Let the candle shine for the beauty of shining.

—Wallace Stevens,
Three Travelers Watch a Sunrise

Contents

The Bar at Twilight

Winter, 1965

In the few months before his story was to appear, he was treated differently at work and at his usual hangouts. The bartender at the White Horse Tavern, himself a yet unpublished novelist, called out his name when he entered the bar and had twice bought him a double shot of rye with a beer back. He had changed in everyone's eyes: He was soon to be a published writer.

And soon a serious editor at a distinguished literary publishing house who had read the story would write him, asking if he had a novel in the works. Which he had. And another one, as well, in a cardboard box on his closet shelf that had made the tour of slush piles as far away as Boston. Only twenty-three, and soon, with the publication of his story in *Partisan Review*, he would enter the inner circle of New York intellectual life and be invited to cocktail parties where he, the youngster, and Bellow and Mary McCarthy, Lowell and Delmore would huddle together, getting brilliantly drunk and arguing the future of American literature.

On the day the magazine was supposed to be on the

stands, he rushed, heart pounding, to the newspaper shop on Sixth Avenue and Twelfth that carried most of the major American literary magazines, pulled the issue of *PR* from the rack, opened it to the table of contents, and found his name was not there. Then, turning the pages one by one, he found that not only was his story not there but neither was there any breath of him.

Maybe he was mistaken; maybe he had come on the wrong day. Maybe the delivery truck had gotten stuck in New Jersey. Maybe he had picked up an old issue. He scrutinized the magazine again: Winter, 1965—the date was right. He went up to the shop owner perched on a high stool, better to see who was pilfering the magazines or reading them from cover to cover and call out, "This is not a library!" He asked the man if this was the most recent issue of *Partisan Review*, and it was, having arrived that morning in DeBoer's truck, along with bundles of other quarterlies that in not too many months would be riding back on that same truck—bound in stacks, magazines no one would ever read.

He took a day to compose himself, to find the right tone before phoning the editor. Should he be casual? "Hi, I just happened to pick up a copy of *PR* and noticed that my story isn't there." Or very casual? "I was browsing through a rack of magazines and remembered that there was supposed to be a story of mine in the recent issue, but it doesn't seem to be there, so I wondered if I had the pub date wrong."

With the distinguished editor's letter in hand—typed and signed and with the praising addendum, "Bravo"—he finally got the courage to call. The phone rang a long time. He hung up and tried again, getting an annoyed, don't-bother-us busy signal. He considered walking over to the office but then imagined how embarrassed he would be, asking, "Excuse me, but I was wondering whatever happened to my story?" Maybe Edmund Wilson would be there behind a desk with a martini in each fist, or maybe the critics Philip Rahv and Dwight Macdonald would be hanging out at the watercooler arguing over the respective merits of Dreiser and Trotsky. What would they make of him and the unimportant matter of his story?

Months earlier, he had written the editor, thanking him, and now he wrote him again: "Might I expect to see my story in the next issue?" To be sure his letter would not go astray, he mailed it at the post office on Fourteenth and Avenue A. And for the next two weeks, he rushed home every day after work to check his mailbox but found no response, just bills and flyers from the supermarket. He knew no one to ask, having no one in his circle remotely connected to *PR* or to any of its writers. For those at the White Horse, he was their ticket to the larger world.

The news that his story had not appeared quickly got around. His colleagues at the Welfare Department—avant-garde filmmakers, artists without galleries, and waiting-to-be-published poets and novelists—where he had been an investigator since graduating from City College in '63, gave him sly, sympathetic looks. "That's a tough break," a poet in his unit said, letting drop that he had just gotten a poem accepted in *The Hudson Review.*

His failure made him want to slink away from his desk the instant he sat down. It was painful enough that he had to go to work there, as it was. It made him queasy the moment he got to East 112th and saw the beige concrete hulk of the Welfare Department with its grimy windows and its clients lining up—eviction notices, termination of utilities letters in hand. His supervisor, who had been at the Welfare Department ever since the Great Depression and who now was unemployable elsewhere, tried to console him, saying he was lucky to be on a secure job track and with a job where he could meet so many different kinds of people with a range of stories, some of which could find their way into his books.

But he didn't need stories. What he needed was the time to tell them. And he had worked out a system to do that. He rose at five, made fresh coffee or drank what was left from the day before, cut two thick slices from a loaf of dark rye, which he bought at that place on Eighth off Second Avenue that sold great day-old bread at half price, and had his breakfast. Sometimes he would shower after breakfast. But the bathtub in the kitchen had no shower, so he had to use a handheld sprinkler, which left a dispiriting wet mess on the linoleum floor, adding cleanup time to the shower itself. Thus, he had a good excuse to cut down on the showers and to use that time at his desk to write.

Usually, by 5:45 A.M., he was dressed and at his desk, the kitchen table he made from crate wood that almost broke the saw in the cutting. He sat at his typewriter for two hours and no matter what had or had not resulted from it, he did not leave the table. At 7:45, he was at the crosstown bus stop on Tenth and Avenue D, and if all went well, he was at the Astor Place station before 8:15 and, if all still went well, he would catch the local and transfer for the express at Fourteenth, get off at Ninety-sixth Street, and take another local to 114th. Then he'd race to clock in—usually a minute or two before nine. It was not good to be late by even a minute. He was still a provisional and had to make a good impression on the Personnel Department.

When he got upstairs to his desk and had joined his unit, he'd look over the list of calls to see if any were urgent. They were all urgent: Someone never got her check because the mailbox had been broken into. Someone was pregnant again. Someone needed more blankets. Someone had had just enough and jumped off the roof on 116th and Park Avenue—her children were at her grandmother's.

Today, he finished all his desk work and phone calls by noon and clocked out for lunch, which he decided to skip. Instead, he finished four field visits very quickly, with just enough time to solicit the information needed to file his reports. He had looked forward all morning to his final, special visit.

He was alarmed when he saw a cop car parked in front of her building. An ambulance, too, with its back doors wide open. He was worried that something bad had happened to her, blind and alone. But the medics were bringing a man down in a stretcher. He was in his eighties, drunk and laughing. The cop spotted his black field book and came over, asking, "Is he one of yours?"

"Not mine," he said.

"Maybe not even God's," the cop said. "His girlfriend shot him in the hand," he added. "Jealousy, at that age!" He laughed. As he was being lifted into the ambulance, the wounded man laughed and said, "Hey! Take me back. I haven't finished my homework."

He rang her doorbell only once before he heard footsteps and then the "Who is it?"

"Investigator," he answered. She opened the door, smiling. She wore white gloves worn at the tips and a long blue dress that smelled of clothes ripening in an airless closet. Her arm extended, her hand brushing along the wall, she led him through a narrow, unlit hall. From her file, which he had reviewed that morning for this visit, he knew it was her birthday. She was eighty-five.

"It's your birthday," he said.

She laughed. "Is that so! I guess I forgot," saying it in a way that meant she hadn't. "I have tea ready," she said.

She poured tea from a porcelain teapot blooming with pink roses on a white sky. Its lip was chipped and stained brown, but the cups and sugar bowl that matched the teapot were flawless and looked newly washed. So, too, the creamy white oilcloth that bounced a dull light into his eyes. It was hot in the kitchen; the oven was on with the door open, though he had told her several times how dangerous that could be. A fat roach, drunk from the heat, made a jagged journey along the sink wall.

"Do you need anything today?" he asked. "Maybe something special?" He wanted to add "for your birthday," but he did not want to press the obvious point. He could put in for a clothes or blanket supplement for her; deep winter was days away. Or a portable electric heater she could carry from one room to another, so she would not have to use the stove. But how would she locate the electric sockets? "Oh! Nothing at all," she said, as if surprised by the question. "Thank you, but what would I need?"

Not to be blind, he thought. Not to be old. Not to be poor. "Well, if anything comes to mind, just call me at the office," he said, remembering then that she had no phone.

"Well," she said shyly. "If you have time, would you read me that poem again?"

She already had the book in hand before he could reply "I'm very glad to." She had bookmarked the Longfellow poem he had read to her during his previous visits.

He read slowly, with a gravity that he thought gave weight to the lines. He paused briefly to see her expression, which remained fixed, serene.

When he finished, she asked him to repeat the opening stanza. "'Tell me not in mournful numbers, / Life is but an empty dream! / For the soul is dead that slumbers, / And things are not what they seem. / Life is real! Life is earnest! / And the grave is not its goal . . .'"

She thanked him and asked, "Do you like the poem?"

"Yes," he said, to please her. But he disliked the poem because of what he thought of as its cloying, sentimental uplift. He did not want to be sentimental but he had to admit how much the lines had moved him anyway.

They sipped tea in silence. He did not like tea but accepted a second cup, commenting on how perfectly she had brewed it. "Come anytime," she said, "It's always nicer to drink tea in company."

She walked him to the door, picking up a cane along the way. He had never seen her use a cane before. He suddenly worried that should she fall and break her hip, alone in the apartment, she could not phone for help. He made a note in his black notebook to requisition a phone for her.

"The cane is very distinguished," he said.

"It helps me hop along." She smiled. "Thank you for reading to me. You have a pleasing voice. Do you sing?"

"My voice is a deadly weapon," he said, surprised by

his unusual familiarity. "Birds fall from the sky on my first note."

"Does it kill rats?" She laughed. "I hear families of them eating in the hall at night."

He fled down the stairs, having once been caught between floors by three young men with kitchen knives who demanded his money, but when they saw his investigator's black notebook, they laughed and said they'd let him slide this time—everyone knew that investigators never carried cash in the field. He sped to the subway, where he squeezed himself into a seat so tight that he could not retrieve his book, Malamud's *The Assistant*, from his briefcase. He tried to imagine the book and where he had left off reading. It was about an old Jewish man who ran a failing grocery store and his assistant, a young Gentile who lugged milk crates and did other small jobs and who stole from him. It was a depressing novel that pained him, but which had, for all its grimness, made him feel he had climbed out of the grocery store's dank cellar and into a healthy sunlight.

The train halted three times. The fourth might be the one where the train got stuck in the blackness for hours, and he thought to get off at the next station and take a bus or run home or, better, close his eyes and magically be there. But, finally, the train lurched ahead, and when he exited at Astor Place, a lovely light early snow had powdered the subway steps. He waited for the bus.

He waited only eight minutes by his watch, but it

seemed an hour, two hours—that he had been waiting his whole life. Finally, he decided to walk and hope to catch the bus along its route. But he still did not see it by the time he got to First Avenue, so he decided to save the fare and walk the rest of the way home to Eighth between C and D. By Avenue A, it began to be slippery underfoot and the snow came down in fists. Now the thought of going home and leaving again in the snowy evening to travel all the way on the snail's pace bus to the White Horse Tavern for dinner seemed a weak idea. Anyway, he was still smarting from the bartender's far-away look and the wisecracks from the bar regulars when he walked in. He decided to eat closer to home, a big late lunch that would keep him through the evening and keep him at home, writing.

Stanley's on Twelfth and B was almost empty, the sawdust still spotless beige. It was early and quiet, with just a few old-timers, regulars from the neighborhood—the crowds his age came after eleven, when he would be in bed. He ordered a liverwurst sandwich on rye with raw onions and a bowl of rich mushroom soup, made in the matchbox kitchen by a Polish refugee from behind the Iron Curtain, an engineer who had to turn cook. A juniper berry topped the soup. That, the engineer told him, was the way you could tell it was authentically Polish. He always searched for the berry after that—like a pearl hiding in the fungus. Stanley, the owner, balder than the week before, brought him a draft beer without his asking. "It's snowing hard," he announced. "Should I salt the street now or later?" He did not wait for an answer and went back to the kitchen to shout at the cook in Polish.

He took two books from his briefcase, so that he could change the mood should he wish: *Journey to the End of the Night*—for the third time—and *Under the Volcano*, which he had underlined and made notes in the margins. "No one writes the sky as does Lowry, with its acid blues and clouds soaked in mescal." He was proud of that note. One day he would write a book of just such notes. Note upon note building to a grand symphony. Then he voted against ever writing such a book, pretentious to its core—worse, it was facile, a cheat. He wanted to write the long narrative, with each sentence flowing seamlessly into another, each line with its own wisdom and mystery, each character a fascination, a novel that stirred and soared. But what was the point of that? What had become of his story?

A girl he liked came in with a tall man in a gray suit. She smiled a warm hello. He returned it with a friendly wave and a smile that he had to force. Now he was distracted and pained and could not focus on reading his book or on his sandwich, which, anyway, was too heavy on the onion. He had met the girl at Stanley's several times, never with a plan, although he had always hoped he would find her there; they talked without flirting, which he was not good at anyway, going directly to the heavy stuff of books and paintings.

The first time he saw her there months earlier, she was reading a paperback of Wallace Stevens's poems. He imagined her sensitive, a poet maybe. She was from upstate, near the Finger Lakes, with their vineyards and soft hills that misted at dawn and had the green look of Ireland. He had never been upstate or to Ireland. He had never been to Europe. She had been, several times, and had spent a Radcliffe year abroad in Paris, where she had sat at the Café de Flore, educating herself after the boring lectures at the Sorbonne in the rue des Écoles. She had learned how to pace herself by ordering *un grand café crème* and then waiting two hours before ordering another, and then ordering a small bottle of Vichy water with *un citron à côté.* By then, she was no more than twenty pages to the end of *La Nausée.* What did he think of Sartre's novel? she had asked him, as if it were a test. He hated it, he said. It crushed him, written as if to prove how boring a novel could be.

"That's smart," she said. "If you were any more original, you'd be an idiot."

They kissed one evening under a green awning on Avenue A. He kissed hungrily, her lips opening him to a new life. After he had walked her to her doorway and gone home and gotten into his bed, he felt as if he just had been released from years in prison, the gates behind him shut, and "the trees were singing to him." He did not have her phone number or her address and, over the next few weeks, when he went to Stanley's, hoping to find her, she was not there.

He buried himself in the Céline and tried not to look at her. But then she was beside him. "Come over, I want you to meet someone," she said, sweetly enough to almost make him forget that there was a someone he was supposed to meet.

"This is George," she said, "my fiancé." He extended his hand and George did the same, a hand that spoke of a law office or some wood-paneled place of business high up—and far downtown, maybe in the Woolworth Building.

George asked him if he'd like a drink, and before he could answer, George called out to Stanley and ordered two double scotches, neat. "Johnnie, Black Label," he said. She was still on her house wine, white, from grapes in California, fermenting under a bright, innocent sky. The drinks came. They had little to say to one another, or if they did, they said little. He made a toast: "Best wishes for your happiness," he said. Not much of a toast, not very original. It would take him a day to think of one better; under the circumstances, perhaps never. He looked at his watch and remembered he had to meet a friend for dinner across town. They all shook hands again, and he wished them both good luck. "You, too, fella," George said.

The snow fell in wet chunks that seemed aimed at

him. When he got home, his head and jacket were wet and he had to brush off the snow married to his trousers. He was worried his jacket would not be dry by morning when he went to work, and he was on the second landing before he realized he had not checked the mail. He thought it was not worth the bother of going back and checking, but he could not stand the thought that he would be home all night wondering if *PR* had finally written him. There was a letter in the mailbox. But it was not from the magazine. But it was also not from Con Edison or Bell Telephone or Chemical Bank, announcing the fourteen dollars in his savings account. When he got to his apartment, he closed the door behind him with a heavy, leaden clunk and slid the iron pole of the police lock into place. "Home is the sailor, home from the sea, and the hunter home from the hill," he announced.

He noticed that his cactus was turning yellow. He had overwatered it, and now it was dreaming of deserts—the old country—as it died slowly, ostentatiously. He thought of getting a cat. It would be great to have company that would be the same as being alone. A black cat that would melt into the night when he slept. He picked up the letter cautiously when he saw there was no return address. It might have come from a disgruntled client who had wanted to spew hatred and threats. But it had not. The note was handwritten, with lots of curls that announced Barnard or Sarah Lawrence or some grassy boarding school in Connecticut.

"Sorry," it said, "that your story did not appear in the new issue as you were led to expect. Do call, if you like." There was a phone number, each digit inscribed as if chiseled in granite and the 7 was crossed. For a moment, he thought it a prank by one of the White Horse crowd, hoping he would call and find he had dialed a funeral parlor or a police station or a suspicious, jealous husband. But what if it was for real?

He washed his face in cold water, brushed his teeth, combed his hair, took four deep breaths, and dialed, holding back for a moment the last digit. At first he thought, with a little lift in his spirits, that it was the girl from the bar. Maybe, after comparing him to her beau, she had decided to call off the engagement. But then he realized how absurd that was, since the girl in the bar had nothing to do with his story. He let the call go through, and on the second ring a woman answered. "I've been calling for a week," she said. "Don't you have a service?"

"I let it go," he said. "Looking for a better one."

"Well, I gave up and wrote you."

"Sorry for the trouble," he said, and then in an anxious rush and hating himself for the rush, he asked, "Are you an editor at *Partisan Review*?"

"Something like that," she said. Then cautiously she added, "We can meet if you like." He wanted to ask if she could tell him right now, over the phone, tell him what had happened to his story, but he held back, not wanting to seem anxious and unsophisticated.

"Sure," he said, adding as casually as he could. "When?"

"How's tonight? I live just across town. You name the place."

"You don't mind coming out in all this snow?" he said, immediately regretting he had asked. What kind of man is afraid of the snow? "I mean, I could come to you if that's easier."

"I'll just grab a cab. How's eight?"

He wondered if she had dinner in mind. He would have to offer to pay for it, and he began calculating his finances. But to his relief, she said, "I'll already have had dinner."

"Okay, then, how's the De Robertis Pastry Shoppe, the café on First, between Tenth and Eleventh, next to Lanza's?"

"Is that the café with the tile walls that looks like a bathroom?"

He didn't like his café being spoken of that way. "I guess some may see it like that."

They fixed the time at 8:30. Just as he was about to ask whether they were going to publish the story in another issue, the line went dead. There were still some hours to go before meeting her and he had time to write or to review the morning's work. The portable Olivetti, shiny red, hopeful, sat quietly where he had left it, waiting patiently on the kitchen table; the two pages he had written beside it, like accomplices. He read over the pages. They were absurd, stupid, illiterate, worthless—and worse, boring. He was stupid and boring, a failure. The Welfare building sailed at him like an ocean liner in the night. "Life is real, life is earnest," he sang as the ship loomed larger.

He did not want to meet her hungry and he did not want to spend money for another sandwich at Stanley's. He scavenged the fridge. The crystal bowl heaped with Russian caviar was not there, so he settled for the cottage cheese, large curd, greening at the top, which he spooned directly from the container. Then he considered taking a nap so he would be refreshed and alert and not stupid or dull but bright when he met her. He practiced a smile but it was strained and pathetic. He tried napping, leaving on the kitchen light so he would not wake in the lonely darkness. The Welfare building pressed full steam toward him, but he blinked it away and tried to clear his mind of all troubling thoughts, but without much success. He rose with the idea of making himself presentable. He brushed his teeth and gave himself a sponge bath; he cleaned his fingernails and brushed his teeth again. He had reached the limit of his toilette and returned to his desk; maybe his pages would brighten at the cleaned-up sight of him; maybe his Olivetti would regard him more favorably and let him turn out some astonishing gems.

By the time he arrived at the café, he had to shake off the heavy snow twice from his umbrella. His shoes were soaked. He had not changed them for fear of getting his second pair drowned as well and thus having to spend the next day at work in wet shoes.

She was easy to spot, sitting in a booth with a pot of tea and a half-eaten baba au rhum. Her black hair was pulled tight in a ponytail; gold hoops dangled from her earlobes; kohl rimmed her eyes; her yellow sweater was the color of straw in the rain. What was she, twenty? She was more Café Figaro on Bleecker, with its Parisian hauteur, than someone who usually came into his neighborhood. He was sure he had spotted her at the White Horse, men hoping to catch her eye circling her table, where she sat in among other men chattering for her attention. She had never once looked up at him, even when he was ostentatiously clutching *Under the Volcano* in his hand.

She smiled in an anxious way that relaxed him and he took his seat and said, "I hope I haven't kept you waiting." He was ten minutes early, but he had no better introductory words. He felt foolish for having said them.

"I liked your story," she said, as if she, too, had mulled over her first words to him and now had let them burst.

"I'm very pleased," he said. *Pleased* seemed tempered and not overanxious, showing a proper balance of self-esteem and of professional dignity. But then he overrode his self-control and said, "Are they still going to publish it?"

She forced a little laugh. "I doubt it."

This was bad news indeed. But before he could ask the cause of this doubt, she said, "He hates me now." She made a high-pitched sound, like a young mouse broken in a trap.

"I read him in college. We all did. I never thought I'd become his assistant! Anyway, he has a new assistant now," she said, her eyes glistening.

Johnny, the café owner, brought over the cappuccino, along with a glass of water and a cloth napkin. He looked at the young woman and smiled and, turning to him, said, "*Hai fatto bene.*"

"You know, it's just one of those crazy things that happens. Maybe not so crazy when people work so closely all the time," she added, as if talking to herself.

He wanted to ask, "Please, what thing that happens?" But he was afraid that pressing her would only make him seem unworldly. Instead, he said, "Yes, crazy things do happen," thinking he would offer, as a current example, the story of the shot man who said he hadn't finished his homework.

The café was foggy, steaming up like the baths on St. Mark's he went to once and hated, all that wet heat boiling his blood—and the absurd thing was that he had to pay to be cooked, too. He could leave now, as he had then, with the steam stripping the skin from his bones. But he was listening to her story and was not ready to run. She looked down. "I suppose you can fill in the rest," she said. And then with a little pinched laugh, she added, "After all, you're the writer." He waited for her to add "and as yet unpublished." But he realized it would have been his addition and not hers and that he was bringing to the table the same feeling of defeat as when he went to the White Horse, where the greetings had gone thin.

"Oh! I don't know," he said with some affected casualness, "I'm not good at realism or office fiction." He was thinking of a popular novel some years back, *The Man in the Gray Flannel Suit*, which he had not read but understood had to do with office politics and unhappy commuters with sour marriages and lots of scotch and martinis before dinner. He knew nothing of that world, making him wonder in what America he lived and if he was an American writer or any kind of writer at all.

She gave him a studied look and in a brisk, businesslike tone said, "Of course, I know that. That's what I like most about your story. I loved that part where a dying blue lion comes into the young blind woman's hut and asks for a bowl of water and how she nurses him to health."

"That sounds a bit corny," he said. "Maybe I should be embarrassed instead of flattered that you remembered it."

He himself had forgotten the passage as well as most of the story. It had seemed so long ago and somewhat like a friend who, for no reason that he knew, had turned on him.

"Don't be silly," she said. "It's an archetype, all archetypes seem corny."

"So," he asked, as if he had not already been told, as if, finally, to invite the coup de grâce, "why won't he publish it?" The steam was clouding him, and the wall's white tiles were oozing little pearls of hot water and bitter coffee.

"Look," she said with an edge in her voice, "I just came to tell you that I'm sorry it didn't work out."

"Excuse me," he said, "I'm a bit slow, more than usual tonight—the steam's getting to me." He wished he could close his eyes and find himself home and, once there, obliterate all memory of the sent story or of having received the acceptance letter that was to have changed his life. The espresso machine was screaming. She looked about the room and then back at him and smiled. "And frankly, I was curious to know what you were like," she said.

"I hope I met your expectations," he said. That was so lame. He started to revise, but she did not give him time.

"My boyfriend also thinks you're a good writer. And he studied with Harry Levin at Harvard."

"Harry Levin's *The Power of Blackness* is a great book." He wanted her to know he knew.

She offered to pay her share of the bill—and a little extra because she had had those two babas au rhum—but he said, in what he thought was a worldly fashion, "Not at all, you are my guest."

He walked her to Ninth and First Avenue and waved for a cab. "Thanks," she said, "I don't believe in cabs, do you? They're so bourgeois." They stood on the corner shivering and waited until the bus skidded to the stop; snow blanketed the roof and the wipers swiped the windshield with maniacal fury. He wanted to kiss her on both cheeks, as he had seen it done in French films, but thought it was too familiar too soon. In any case, the hood of her slicker covered much of her face. She smiled at him very pleasantly, he thought. On the second step of the nearly empty bus, she turned and said, "I don't have a boyfriend." He waited until he saw her take her seat. He waved as the bus moved into the traffic, but she was facing away and did not see him.

He thought of returning to the café, but he was sick of coffee and the screaming white tiles, or of going back to Stanley's bar for a beer, but he was afraid he would run into the girl he had liked—still liked—and she would ask what he had thought of her fiancé and he would have to be brave and swallow it and say how solid he seemed and how he was happy for her if she was happy.

He went home and climbed the stairs. A dog barked at him behind a door on the second floor—Camus, *The Stranger*, the mistreated, beaten dog; the Russian woman on the third floor was boiling cabbage and the hall smelled of black winter and great sweeps of bitter snow, a branchless tree here and there dotting the white expanse—Mother Russia, Dostoyevsky, *Crime and Punishment*, the bloody ax, a penniless student. On the fourth floor, not a peep. Then suddenly, a groan followed by a cry like a man hit with a shovel: "*Welt welt,* kiss *mein tuchas.*"

On the fifth floor, he thought about the groan and the cry on the fourth. He had seen the tattooed numbers on the old man's wrist and knew what had given them birth—hills of eyeglasses, mounds of gold teeth, black, black smoke rising from an exhausted chimney. When he finally reached the sixth and last floor, he stopped at his door, key in hand, thinking to turn and leave the building again for a fresh life in the blizzard. But he was already shrouded in snow and was chilled and wanted to take off his clothes and lie in bed and be whoever he was. There was a song coming from the adjacent apartment: Edith Piaf, who regretted nothing.

His playboy neighbor had returned from Ibiza with a sack full of 45s and a deep suntan. He always had visitors, girls from Spain and Paris and London, who came to crash and who sometimes stayed for a week or two. One had knocked at his door at two in the morning and asked if he had any coke. He apologized, saying he did not drink soda; she made a face and said, "Where're you from?" Another banged at his door at five in the morning blind drunk; she had mistaken his apartment for the playboy's. "You have the wrong door," he said, his sleep shattered. "Who cares," she said, staggering into his room.

He was down to his shorts and T-shirt and had pulled a khaki surplus army blanket to his knees. He sat up in bed with Céline and read. Ferdinand was working in an assembly line in Detroit. Molly was his girlfriend. Ferdinand was a young French vagabond, and she was a prostitute. She loved him. There was no loneliness in the world like the loneliness of America. The two had made a fragile cave of paper and straw against the loneliness. He read until he no longer knew what he was reading. Then he gave up. His mind was elsewhere and nowhere. The day had been fraught with distractions. He was a distraction. He thought of phoning someone. Maybe the assistant he had just left at the snowy bus stop—to find out if she got home all right. Maybe he would call some friends, but he did not know whom and, finally, he did not have anyone he wanted to talk with or who would welcome his call. He thought again of getting a cat. A white one he could see in the dark. The cactus looked healthier in the lamplight; maybe it had had second thoughts and decided to give life another try. "Good night," he said to himself and switched off the light.

But he quickly turned it back on, thinking again of calling the assistant, thinking that perhaps they could soon become friends. They could go to poetry readings at the Y—Auden and other great poets read there—or take in a movie at the Thalia on Broadway and Ninety-fifth—he was sure she liked foreign films, like Fellini's *La Strada*, or Bergman's *The Seventh Seal.* Maybe on the weekends they would sit over coffee under the bronze shadow of Rodin's giant Balzac in MoMA's tranquil garden and he would read to her his latest work. She would immediately recognize what was excellent and what was not and, with her as his editor and muse, he would write beautiful, original stories and novels. She had already been his champion. Now they would collaborate, nourishing each other on life's creative adventure and they would never be lonely in Detroit or anywhere else. He tried to remember if he had found her attractive, but she was a blur with a messenger's voice.

Maybe he had neglected to see that she was desirable. He suspected that she was. He was sure of it. Maybe he'd invite her for a dinner of spaghetti and salad and house red at Lanza's, where whatever you wanted on the menu they did not have. Maybe at dinner together there, under the frescoes of Sicilian villas grilling in the sun, she would find its prix fixe and soiled menus louche and seductive and thus find him equally, if not more, so. Maybe one morning they would wake together in his bed, the raw light from the window on her beautiful, bare, straight shoulders. Maybe one midnight, after a movie and over coffee and a plate of rolls at Ratner's on Second Avenue and under the eyes of the shaking old Jewish waiters, retired from the Yiddish Theatre, they would realize they were in love. Maybe they were already in love.

He could hear the scraping of a snow shovel in the

distance—maybe on Avenue C. His own street would not be cleared for days. He went to his window. The synagogue across the way had been locked tight for two years, its smashed windows covered with sheets of fading plywood. The grocery three buildings to the east of him was closed—the two brothers who owned it were still on Rikers Island for fencing radios—so the whole way to Avenue D might be snowed over, impeding his walk to the crosstown bus on Tenth and D. The snow was building on his window ledge and he would let it mount, better to gauge how much of it was piling up below in the street he could no longer clearly see. With all this snow, the morning bus might be delayed, and the subway, too. He would have to get up extra early to get to work, and budget himself the time to shovel Kim's sidewalk. The laundry was still dark; Kim was in the back recovering from a mugging and beating three days earlier. "Where is your gold?" the robbers had demanded. "Chinks always have gold," one said, giving Kim a whack on the knee with a blackjack. He would have to shovel the snow for him before he went to work, or Kim would get a summons or two. When would he find time to write? Who cared if he did? He would go down in the street and sleep there in the blanketing snow, Céline in hand. Or maybe the Lowry.

He went back to bed, tossing and turning and sleeping a dozen minutes at a time, then waking. He returned to Céline. Ferdinand was still miserable in cold Detroit, but he had no luck in focusing on the Frenchman's misery and no better luck with *Under the Volcano*, whose drunken protagonist still reeled about in the hot Mexico sun. He went to the window again. The snow had piled a quarter way up the window and was whirling in the sky like it owned the world. He might be late to work or never get there no matter how early he left his house.

There was a knock at the door, alarming at that hour, but then he thought it was his playboy neighbor or one of his wandering drunk girlfriends, or the one always prowling for drugs. He opened the door to the limit of the chain. It was the neighbor, drink in hand.

"I heard you puttering about and thought it was not too late." He opened the door, feeling vulnerable in his underwear.

"Just wanted you to know I'm moving out and want to sublet for a year or so. Thought you might like it for your office." He could not afford two apartments, scraping by on one, but he said, "Thanks, give me a day or so to think about it."

"The rent's the same thirty-two a month—I'm not trying to make anything on it."

"I wouldn't have thought so." It was cold in the hallway and he thought to invite him in but was embarrassed that he would see three days' worth of dishes still piled up in the sink. And then, feeling he was not cordial enough, he added, "Where're you going?" expecting him to say Ibiza or Paris or San Francisco.

"Uptown, closer to work."

"Sorry you're leaving," he said.

"Well, me, too. But Dad thinks it's time to put on the harness, and he got me something in publishing."

"Oh!"

"It should be okay. I'm told editors mostly go to lunch."

"I've heard that," he said. He wanted to add, "I'll send you my novel; maybe you'll like it." But he felt humiliated and hated himself for the thought that he would ask.

"Come and lunch with me one day!"

"I'd like that," he said. They shook hands. He shut and locked the door but felt he was on the outside, in the hall, freezing. He checked his Timex. How had it ever become midnight? No wonder he was freezing—at that hour, the boiler was shut off and all the radiators turned to ice. He lit the oven, setting it on low, and left the door open. Maybe he would buy a portable heater and one for the blind woman. Maybe he'd drag out the Yellow Pages from the back of the closet and look up the closest animal shelter, like the ASPCA, which he'd heard was respectable. He would go there on Saturday and would come home that very day with a cat. He wondered what kind of cats they had there. Old ones, sick ones, mean ones, dirty and incontinent ones who would pee on his bed, all ready to be gassed. He would save ten and lead them in a herd to follow him as he went from room to room. He'd circle them around his bed at night and keep away Bad Luck. He had Bad Luck. He'd save fifteen. Seven white ones; seven black ones. The other would be marmalade. Would they let him take that many at one time?

He could not sleep. But he could not stay awake another minute. Better than chancing a morning bus and subway failure, maybe he'd get dressed and start walking to work now, fording the snowdrifts so to be sure to get there on time. He'd show up at first light, half frozen, waiting for the doors to open. He would be exemplary. He would be made permanent. He would be promoted and never have time to write again or wait for rejections in the mail. Or maybe he would be found icy dead at the foot of the Welfare Department's still-closed doors. The editor of *Partisan Review* would eventually learn of his heroic death and publish his story, boasting that he had been their promising discovery.

The snow had bullied the streets into silence. The building slept without a snore. Tugboats owlishly hooted in the distance as they felt their way in the blinding snow. He closed his eyes. He stayed that way for several minutes, chilled under his blanket. But then the oven slowly heated, sending him its motherly warmth. He rose and went to the kitchen table and to the gleaming red Olivetti waiting for him there.

The Veranda

SHE'S ON A VERANDA FRONTING A BEACH cut short by the bandit tide. The sea beyond, its mysteries and waves, she's used to them, but then again, she never is. Those waves pillaging the shore each day. From time to time, she glances at the single white rose on the table. The same crystal vase as always, a different rose each day, but always from the same garden, hers. A Bach partita—winter light in a faded mirror—flows through the open French doors. She's reading Marcus Aurelius again, and again finds comfort in the obvious: To lessen the pains of living, one must diminish desire for the material world, its promises and illusions.

There is a polite rustle at the door. Michelos, the butler—who else would it be?—with a silver pot of coffee wrapped in a linen napkin. He nods. She smiles for thanks.

Michelos is old. He has seen her through three husbands, two of whom had married her for her money. The first husband died mid-sentence at breakfast—a sentence she had no wish for him to complete, in any case, because it concerned his allowance and the need for its substantial increase.

She was young when she first married and still young when her husband left her, the planet, his bespoke suits, handcrafted shoes, and the beige cashmere socks he so cherished and had kept rolled in ten cedar-lined drawers. She had come to dislike him not only because she had gradually understood that he had married her principally for her wealth but also because she found his sartorial desires, like his lovemaking, so conventional.

The second husband, on understanding that her wealth was not to flow endlessly into the mansion's garages, flooded with his custom-made cars, and who considered Bentleys and Rolls-Royces mere Fords, left her for an older woman who appreciated the elegant way he mixed cocktails and chattered with her guests at dinner parties, and who was willing to pay for his ever-increasing automotive needs.

The last husband, who was fifty-eight when they married and who made her happy well into her mid-forties, drowned in the same ocean she was now regarding with tenderness and fear. At breakfast one morning together, as every summer morning, he kissed her, a deep kiss on the mouth and not just a husbandly peck. Then he was off for his usual swim. He waved to her from far away in the ocean and then he was gone. He was the love of her life.

❖

He was an artist. Not very famous but not unrecognized. He was appreciated, respected, living modestly on the sale of his paintings, which unabashedly had roots in Poussin and Cézanne. Like them, he searched for the immortal structure beneath and underlying the painting in whatever subject it represented. Like them, his life was a consecration to art and a daily presence to its fulfillment. (He, however, would have been shy about such words as *consecration.*) "You cannot know what the work will look like unless you show up for it" was the way he put it. He made no fuss about being dedicated to his art and he did not feel superior to those artists without similar devotion. But he did not spend time in their company, either.

He lived decently and did not require much to do so—a small loft that he had bought for a song in the early sixties, in a building now a condo and a warren of billionaires, was all he needed and wanted for shelter and work. He had no retreat by the sea or elsewhere as had many of his colleagues. I say *colleagues* because he did not have friends in the full sense of the word, though he believed in the idea of friendship as found in the essays of Montaigne. He liked the idea so much that he did not attempt to injure it through experience. He stayed in the city through the hottest summers on the deadest weekends, when no one but tourists and the homeless roamed the burning streets. In the spring and into the late fall, he walked to the park on the lower East River and read on a bench fronting the watery traffic of tugs and barges. A white yacht on its way to Florida or the Caribbean might pass by and someone might wave. In winter, he kept in, breakfasted on Irish oatmeal and coffee and then more coffee; he often skipped lunch and ate bread in torn hunks and drank coffee: two sugars, three ounces of milk. At night, he dined at an Italian restaurant with so-so food on the corner of his street. It had a green awning in summer, and you could sit under it in the rain.

Sometimes one of the young female assistants from his gallery found a pretext to visit him. He was friendly, solicitous, but did not mix business with sex. He imagined the resulting complications, the discomfort of going to his gallery and facing a woman he had slept with a few times but in whom he had no deeper interest. And he did not welcome the discomfort he imagined for her or the awkwardness of his circumspect dealer of fifteen years, who never mixed business with anything if he could help it.

He liked the city, he liked solitude, he liked going and coming when he wished; he liked sleeping and waking in his own bed. He liked women, but mostly on a certain basis: that they did not want to live with him, did not want to have children, did not want to call him at any hour they chose to chat; that they did not like or affect to like sports; that they did not buy or urge him to buy new clothes, to get a haircut, a shave, or have his nails trimmed, though he always kept them trimmed and his face shaved and hair cut short. The women he liked did not or needed not to work. This excluded many women, even those women of leisure married to wealth, because he considered their marriage a job, a fancy one without regular hours or a visible paycheck, but a job nonetheless. In any case, he did not sleep with married women, first out of principle—the one that has to do with not hurting people—and the other because he was selfish about his time and did not wish to squander it on clandestine arrangements and their inevitable time-consuming and emotional complications.

He liked women who read books he honored: He was snobbish about that but did not care that he might be thought so. The books one read were as telling as the friends one chose. You could be fooled or betrayed by friends but never by books. Plato, for example, always stayed faithful and always gave more than he received. Proust could be relied on for his nature descriptions, especially flowers bordering paths through luxuriant gardens. He loved gardens because of Proust but felt he need not visit any because he had seen and walked through enough of them in the Frenchman's world. He used this as an excuse to get out of visiting his collectors in Connecticut, who prided themselves on their gardens, their endless yards of rose beds, especially.

He liked above all women who loved painting. He did not care for them as much if they liked sculpture, because he did not care for sculpture, except for smallish items such as Mycenaean heads and masks from Côte d'Ivoire, very abstract and synthetic. In short, he liked sculpture the starker and the more minimal the better. He disliked mostly everything else ever deconstructed or assembled and felt antipathy for the grand posture and thus disdained Rodin's figures in particular among the moderns. Everything, in fact, after the time of Pericles he found dreary and dead, the stuff to fill old movie palace lobbies. He once wrote in his notebook that we need not bother to fill empty space with sculpture—any natural rock formation is better than any sculpture, so, too, trees. Deserts do not need sculpture; emptiness is their point and their beauty.

About painting he had no illusions. He did not believe in its social or psychological or spiritual transformative powers. He did not believe that there is progress in art or in civilization. All great, significant art was timeless and equal in value—in beauty. Beauty was the end and reason for all art, period.

He had few extravagances. But he would travel long distances to revisit paintings he loved and he would make, with great planning, expeditions to places holding paintings he admired. He spent two weeks alone at the Ritz Hotel in Madrid so that he could walk across the road after breakfast and before dinner to look at

Velazquez's *Las Meninas,* which he considered the greatest painting ever made after the sixteenth century. His certainty about this annoyed other artists, who saw in it an inflexibility of taste that might be applied to his judging their own work. They were also put off by his unwillingness to consider that no single work of art is the "greatest." Sometimes, for fun, he would seem to concede the point and say, "Well, it is the first greatest among equals."

He once trailed a beautiful woman after seeing her studying with great intensity a painting by Picasso in a hall at the Louvre. He followed her into a room of Poussins and was pleased to see her fixed on one painting, *Echo and Narcissus,* for several full minutes. That she might have seen the affinity between the two artists intrigued him and she increased in stature and thus grew more and more interesting by the minute. Then she seemed to take a different track altogether when she went into other rooms and gave her attention to a canvas by Perugino and then later focused on a painting by Parmigianino. He was a bit let down. It occurred to him that she was progressing or governed along no aesthetic insight or principle but merely visiting artists whose surnames began with the letter *P.*

He followed her to the museum's café, where she sat alone by the window facing a vast courtyard and Paris beyond. He sat at the table closest to her and took his time ordering *un grand crème* and a tartine with butter—exactly what she had requested and what finally was brought to them both. She spoke to the waiter in a French from an earlier day, when words were sounded in their fullness. She would have made a great actress on the seventeenth-century stage, reciting Racine or Corneille. For all that, he wasn't sure he liked the elevated, rich, overeducated, worldly, superior tone of her voice. But then he liked it—he supposed her to be French and thus she could sound as fancy and superior as she wished, or why else be French? He glanced her way, hoping to make eye contact, but she had pulled a book out of her bag—expensive, smooth, trim, no frills, oxblood red, with a narrow strap—and engaged herself in its lines.

He was shy except with women, from whom he would gamble rebuff, even rebuke, to meet. His theory was that the chance of knowing an interesting woman was more important than any rejection, and since his advances were soft-spoken and courteous, his politeness was met with the like or, at worst, with a little coldness born of natural suspicion and wariness.

"Look," he said, taking the chance that she knew English. "I understand your interest in the connection between Poussin and Picasso, but I don't see your leap to Parmigianino, a fine artist but irrelevant to what connects the other two."

She gave him a long look. Almost scientific in its disinterestedness. Then in a pleasant but firm voice and in an English more beautiful than her French, she said,

"I'm married. Happily or unhappily is another matter, but married and obedient to all its obligations and injunctions and oaths."

"Lamentably so," he replied, not sure exactly what he meant.

She drank her coffee slowly, looking at the sea, its thick swell and sullen heaviness. It covered the world. It raided its shores, carrying trees and husbands in its teeth. One day the sea would gallop over the dunes and drag her into its watery camp. But if she chose, she would not wait for it to come to carry her away and she would take a long swim from which she would never again step onshore.

She had walked into his gallery cold, looking for a watercolor by Marin and a painting by Hartley she knew were being offered there. It was an old-fashioned gallery she felt comfortable visiting because the owner kept his distance, did not make too much fanfare about his artists or their work.

The gallery specialized in early to mid-twentieth-century American art; thus he was in the company of Walt Kuhn, Kuniyoshi, Fairfield Porter, artists he admired, although they were too tame for him, never reaching beyond the literal. He was sometimes fearful that that was also true of him, too tame, too literal, and whenever he got sufficiently worried, he took the train to the Philadelphia Museum of Art and for a full half hour stood in front of Cézanne's large *Bathers.* He would grab a sandwich in the museum's café and let his mind go nowhere; then he'd return to the painting and start absorbing it again. He would come home feeling purified and try to purge his work of the superfluous without eliminating areas that gave his painting its valuable subtext and life. He strove.

He had been approached by galleries more important and chic than his, ones that had offered him monthly stipends and lavish catalogues written by distinguished critics whose names would give added weight to his reputation, galleries that had juice in the art market and could inject oil into its machinery.

But he liked his gallery, having been invited to join it when he was still unknown; he stayed loyal to the man who had the intelligence to understand his work and to act on it—to put his money where his taste was. He found in the dealer a man not too chummy and not too remote and who quietly and successfully did his job of promoting and selling his few living artists. He liked also that his dealer always wore modest pinstripe suits and bow ties, and that he went to the Oak Room at the Plaza at 5:30 every weekday and drank a dry martini and then, in nasty weather, took the Madison Avenue bus uptown to his home and to his wife of thirty years.

She bought the Marin watercolor and, undecided,

put a hold on the Hartley. Then the dealer asked if she would be interested in seeing the work of an artist he had long admired and long represented, and he took her into his office. He had spoken to her of this artist before, but she had not made the effort to see the work. The three paintings in the dealer's office unnerved, then calmed her, as if she at last had found her map home after being lost for years in a faraway country whose language she did not understand and could never learn. Musical they were, these paintings, in melancholic counterpoint with death. By what alchemy did paint become music?

She did not know who he was, had never seen his photograph, as he shunned having his face in the catalogues of his shows—there were no catalogues, in any case. His picture had never appeared in any of the art magazines she subscribed to, which, with the exception of the bulletin from the Metropolitan Museum of Art, where she was a trustee, were none.

She bought one painting, asking that she remain anonymous. Then, two weeks later, after the first painting's music had occupied her dreams, she returned and bought another.

Weeks later, she sent the artist an unsigned note of appreciation via his gallery. He answered, through his gallery, with a handkerchief-size drawing—in the mode and friendly parody of Poussin—of a tree on fire and a medieval battlement in the distance also in flames. She withdrew, feeling the heat of his closeness and the threat of disappointment. (Better never to get too close or meet an artist whose work you admire, because all artists are inferior to their work.) She wrote back, thanking him politely for the drawing—and then, in a rush of feeling, added some heartfelt lines on what she loved about his work. She feared those lines would be misunderstood and open doors better left shut, but she also felt that a polite mere thank-you would not have expressed the fullness of her, of her emotions. She knew she was equivocating, because her letter might suggest that while her doors were shut, they were also unlocked.

He responded a day later. Come, his note said, to his studio and choose a watercolor.

While the principle never to meet the artist remained true, she also wanted to meet him, if nothing else than to confirm the principle—a lie. She wanted to meet him because she wished to like him, to be moved by him, to have him move her. She wanted to believe that the untroubled purity she found in his paintings mirrored his own distinguished soul. She thought she might be disappointed should she ever meet him, and she was pained by her longing for someone perfect or someone whose very imperfections and failures she would find noble.

In short, after some days of indecision, she went to his loft. She had her car and chauffeur wait in the street should she decide on a quick getaway. They smiled both comfortably and uncomfortably. They chitchatted some minutes and, much to her own surprise, she asked if he lived alone.

"Lamentably," he said.

She laughed. "You seem fond of that word."

He nodded. And slyly said, "Regrettably."

"What if I said I'm still married? What would you say to that?"

"That should you leave this room, I would lament you."

"Then perhaps I won't leave."

She gave her driver the day off. He was glad for the reprieve. She stayed there in the artist's loft until the next morning, when they both went to breakfast—the scrambled eggs were cut into white strings, the bacon was undercooked and burnt at the same time, and the coffee was tar hauled from a back road in Tennessee—in a dim diner by the Hudson River favored by truckers and taxi drivers and artists of that era.

"And what about God?" she asked. "Where are you on that?" She was still young enough to think about and to ask such questions. In any case, she was not asking about God; she was probing to discover his weak spot, and having found none after hours of talking, finally, at 2:38 in the morning, when he said, "It's time," she followed him to his bed.

For the first several months of their years together, they divided themselves between his loft and her apartment, from whose windows they could see Central Park and the Plaza Hotel. They shared breakfast at six, after which he vanished in a taxi to his studio downtown and spent the day painting. If by seven that evening he felt not ready to leave his work, he'd phone her and they would or would not meet again for dinner, or they would or would not meet again that night, in which case he'd sleep alone, but she would come downtown at six to breakfast with him at the diner with the bad food. The string eggs, burnt bacon, and tar coffee had worked into their history. Or sometimes she would appear with a full breakfast, silver service and all, her chauffeur and maid and herself toting platters and coffeepots up to her husband's loft. Then she might linger awhile after they had sipped their last cup of coffee and go to his bed.

He had been painting with a new vigor and insight, which his dealer recognized immediately. There was also a certain charity, a kind of generosity lacking earlier while still keeping the work within its usual reserved boundaries. "Love does its wonders," the dealer said dispassionately but with a conviction born from romantic memories of his youth, when he first met his wife.

Everything seemed in balance, so the dealer was upset when he learned that she was building a house in Montauk. "Why go out there in the first place?" the dealer asked her.

"For the calm and the air and the sea," she replied. "He's too old to spend summers broiling in the city. I'll build him a studio he won't want to leave. A place he and every other artist has only ever dreamed of."

The dealer had seen artists appear from the mist and then vanish from the scene; he had seen exalted reputations fall into the mud—or, even worse, just melt away slowly into oblivion. And not always because the work had changed for the worse. The moment had changed and the artist was no longer in that moment but suddenly somewhere else, far away, in the land of the forgotten and fruitlessly awaiting the day to be rescued and brought home again with honors.

But sometimes, their flame went out because the hungry fuel that had fed it was no longer there, and the rich life took its place. He knew artists who, when they reached the pinnacle of their art and reputation and had earned vast sums, turned out facsimiles of their earlier, hard-earned work and were more concerned with their homes, trips, social calendars, their placement at dinner parties than with anything that might have nourished their art, which coasted on its laurels.

And for that last reason, the dealer said to her, "Go slow and keep the life contained, for his sake and yours."

She laughed. "Don't worry, no one will come to our dinner parties, should we ever give them, and we shall not go if ever asked."

"This is not a moralistic issue," he said. "And I'm not against money. You know it's not about you. I love you," he said, turning red.

"And I love you for how you were in his life and in his work from the start."

He made an exaggeratedly alarmed face and said, "Were?"

"Were, are, and always will be," she said, then repeated it.

They left on good terms. He apprehensive of what was to become of his artist; she concerned that in trying to make a gracious life for her husband she might be digging their cushioned graves.

Now he was dissolved in the sea, vanished in a soup of bones and brine. And now she was alone until the sea took her away, too, if it were the sea that one day would be her executioner. Until that time, she would remain alone with the butler, who in time would tremble and whose hand would spill the coffee and let the morning rose fall. Then, one day, he would tremble all over and, after the back-and-forth of hospitals, he would be gone. Then she would sit on the veranda and face the sea and listen to music, maybe some somber cello pieces from Marais or Saint-Colombe or Bach—music on a small scale, where, atomlike, the energy of beauty compresses.

Eventually, she would answer the phone and seem delighted that a friend had called to invite her to dinner. An elegant dinner with distinguished guests—an ambassador who had written a memoir, a former editor of a venerable publishing house, a novelist always mentioned for the Nobel Prize, two widows who funded the arts, a young poet who would have preferred not to be there but who understood the draw and use of powerful people—all affable and solicitous of her. The food, a poached wild salmon with sorrel, would be excellent, the wine even better. The conversation would flow with delicacy and nuance, with worldly authority. But not one word said the whole evening would approach her heart.

She would be home by eleven and sit and read in an old leather chair he had loved. The lazy cat would curl about her ankles and fall asleep. She herself would start to doze off—as she got older, fewer and fewer books held her interest. Only Proust still spoke to her, an old, intimate friend with long, twisting sentences whose fineness still absorbed her and kept her feeling grateful for his visit. She left her gardens to the gardeners, who went wild with the freedom, each planting to his own vision. Rose beds rushed against walls of blue hydrangeas; a field of yellow daffodils invaded a stand of black tulips. The grass went from tame to wild without transition. She enjoyed the anarchy and the disorder, but it delivered only so much pleasure and then the excitement went flat. People also went stale quickly. The interesting ones, the ones with character and who had struggled to make their place in the world, had died. She was too tired and too far away in time to meet their replacements, if there were any.

He had left her everything. His clothes, of course, a closet full of khakis and pairs of brown loafers worn down at the heels; one pair of black shoes, soles and heels as good as new; one suit, gray pinstripe, hardly worn, made for him in London, where he had once spent a week drunk on museums; three sports jackets, two for winter, a red-and-green plaid for summer; two dress shirts to be adorned with a tie, the rest just blue cotton button-downs. Apart from the art, and there was little of that, she prized his notebooks, some filled with sketches like the one he had sent her years earlier and some with jottings and notes and quotes from the reading he loved.

He wrote about the *Bathers*, how he loved the awkwardness of the nude figures, the almost childish painting of their forms. As if Cézanne had set out to fail. As if he had sought through that failure a great visual truth at once obvious and occult. He quoted from a letter of Cézanne's in which he spoke about his unfinished paintings—paintings he had deliberately left unfinished, patches here and there of raw canvas as if left to be painted later. Cézanne had found truth in their incompleteness. That the empty spaces invited color, leaving the viewer to imagine that color, leaving the viewer his exciting share in the completing of the visual narrative; blank spaces suggesting also that art, like life, does not contain all the information and that it is a lie when it pretends so.

Silence, except for the churning sea. The sea is high, just some fifty yards from her, black and cold. The house, too vast for one, feeling the sea's chill, gives a shudder. She gives a shudder. Then she makes her way up the stairs to her too-large room and her too-large bed, under a too-high ceiling, and she waits for the sea—having taken from her everything else—to come crawling to her window like a bandit hungry for silver.

The Snow on Tompkins Square Park

A MAN LIMPED INTO A BAR. He folded his stubby hands on the counter. The bartender, Aloysius, a blue horse, said, "What will you have?"

"A glass of water, please."

"We serve horses here, and people who look horsey. You aren't and you don't."

"I'm waiting for my girlfriend, she's very horsey."

"Well, in that case," the bartender said, "cool your heels."

The man waited a few minutes, checked his watch, looked out the window. Freezing rain fell outside. He nursed his water and then, twenty-seven minutes later, when the glass was dry, he said, "I guess she's not coming. Or she got stuck in the rain."

"Wait a while longer," the bartender said. "You don't want her to come and find you gone."

He had been thinking the same thing, but he also thought he would leave and give her a lesson for always being late and expecting him to be waiting. Or if she did not come at all, he could pretend he had never been there. But the icy rain made him decide he would stay. It gave him a good excuse to tarry.

"Thanks," the man said. He wanted to give weight to his "thanks" and added, "Very sporting of you."

He moved to the edge of the bar to make space for other customers, but none seemed to be coming. He looked about the room. A table of three horses. They looked at him, not unfriendly but not friendly, looked at him in a dispassionate way, he thought. One horse, a red filly, gave him a warm smile, showing him all her teeth. Some were drinking a dark beer in glass buckets and there were bowls of oats set on each table, but no one was eating.

The bar had no TV and no radio. The woman he was waiting for made him unhappy. She had always made him unhappy; she would always make him unhappy. That thought made him say, "I'd like a scotch."

"Sure," the bartender said.

"And make it a double, neat."

"We have all kinds of scotches," the bartender said.

The man looked into his wallet and said, "Nothing too expensive and nothing too cheap, if you have."

The horse gave him a long stare with one eye. "That's okay, you don't need to order anything. I'll bring you another glass of water, with a lemon twist this time if you want."

"Yes, I'd like that," the man said. "And the scotch, too, please." He looked at his stubby, hairy fingers, counting each one twice. He looked in the mirror behind the rows of glowing, friendly bottles and saw that nothing of him looked horsey but that he looked, rather, like a flounder.

After silently counting his fingers again and letting his thoughts roam, he heard a voice from one of the tables.

"Hey! If you're alone, come over and join us, why don't you," the red filly said.

He glanced at the bartender, who said, "That's fine. I'll bring over your drink."

The man introduced himself. The others did the same. One, who looked like he had a thoughtful life, was named Jake. The other, with a black patch over his eye, was named Patch, and the red filly said her name was Red.

"Someone stand you up?" she asked.

He stood up and sat down again. "It seems like it. Yes, someone."

"What brings you to these parts, Louis?"

"I live up the street, on the park."

"Never seen you here," the filly said.

"I heard we weren't welcome."

"Everyone's welcome who looks a little horsey or is sympathetic to horses or hasn't injured them. Have you?"

"No, I like horses. Thought I would like to be one. But I guess I can't because I look like a flounder."

They laughed. "That's very funny," Jake, the wise-looking horse, said. "But you don't look like a flounder, you look more like a . . . like a codfish!"

Then Patch said, "Doesn't matter what fish you look like, you look like a fish out of water."

"Yes, I'm a fish out of water. I don't know where the water is."

"I think you need to be cheered up a bit," the filly said. "Have another drink."

"That's a good idea," Louis said. "One's on the way." He called out to the bartender.

Two horses walked in, one very large, broad, and meaty, with a cocky walk; the other lean and shy, with his head down. They came to the table. The cocky one said, "Who's this fella?"

"A friend," the filly said.

The large horse gave him an intimidating look, then said to the filly, "Whatya doing later?"

"I don't know, Harry," she said. "It's not later yet."

"Okay, okay." He laughed it off. "I'll be here awhile and catch you later. You, too, fella," he said. He took his time getting to the bar, the shy one trailing behind.

"Don't mind him," Red said. "He used to be a police horse. He was very proud of himself when he was younger. He was big in the Macy's Day Parade and the Easter Day parade and the Columbus Day parade and all the important parades and now he's retired, with a nice pension."

"I didn't mind him," Louis said.

Patch, who had been silent until then, said, "Don't mind him but watch out when he starts backing into you, because soon he'll have you squeezed against a wall and you'll wonder what happened to your breath. He learned lots of nasty tricks for all kinds of occasions."

The bartender brought over a half-filled tall glass of scotch and a glass of water with a twist of lemon. "Be anything else?"

"Not right now," Louis said, looking about him. He smiled and raised his glass in a toast to his new companions. "To horses," he said.

The wise horse tapped his hoof on the table and said to the bartender, "Bring him a bag of oats—no, make it a bowl. And don't forget a spoon."

A yellow horse with long eyelashes sauntered into the bar solo. She came to the table and daintily made her hellos.

"Hello, Sally," Red said. "Haven't seen you in a while."

"Well, I've been here and there," she said. "Mostly there, if you get my drift." She gave the man a long, friendly look and smiled, showing a row of large white teeth.

"Introduce me to your friend, why don't ya?"

"This is Louis," Red said. "He owns a few banks and a string of polo ponies."

"Hey! That's great," Sally said. "See you later, Mr. Banker."

She left and brushed up to the police horse. They

chattered amiably. Affably. The police horse said loudly, "Bring Sally a kir royale."

Red turned to the man and, sotto voce, said, "She had her teeth done, can't you tell? Anyway, she used to be a circus horse. Very famous and loved by persons from six to sixty! She had the riders stand on her bare back, and she'd circle faster and faster but no one ever fell off."

"That's wonderful," Louis said, his thoughts traveling elsewhere. "Fish out of water," he said dreamily. "What's the water I belong to? The Atlantic, the Pacific, the Mediterranean, the Nile, the Amazon, the Hudson?"

"You could swim in the East River," Jake said. "It's so close, you could walk right over and dive in."

"Cod don't swim in the East River," Patch said.

"Well, they used to swim in the Hudson two hundred years ago," the wise horse said. "It's an estuary, you know."

Everyone nodded. Aloysius called out, "A river drowned in an ocean."

"You know, the longer you sit here, the less you look like a fish and the more you look like a horse," Red said.

"How kind," Louis said.

"Yes," the wise horse said, "that's true. I see equine features emerging. Maybe because I see Red, our friend here, likes you."

"Oh! Go on," she said with a huff.

"I'm sorry, think I have intruded on something here," said Louis.

"But nothing that can't be resolved, right, Red?" the wise horse said.

The filly tossed her head and said, "Look! It's stopped raining." And, turning to Louis: "Maybe you'd like to go for a walk?"

"Think I could use one. Think I'm getting a little tipsy." He let his head fall to one side. He laughed. He called out to the bartender, "If a woman comes in looking for me, offer her a drink and ask her to wait, okay? A kir royale, maybe."

The bartender nodded. The police horse turned swiftly and said, "That's my signature drink. Go find another, chum."

"Don't even answer him," the filly said. "Let's just go."

And they went into the day.

The day was gray. A chilled gray. The sky was thickening with crystals of gray light. He was gray.

Tompkins Square Park was empty but for a lone policeman, statuelike, in a glistening rain slicker.

"Let's cut through here," she said, stepping into the walk on Eighth and Avenue B.

"I never knew they let horses in the park," he said, stopping short.

"They don't," she said, "but the cop's a friend."

"How ya doing, Red?" the cop said. "Still looking for work?"

"Not anymore," she said. "My horse came in."

The cop looked at the man, up and down.

"Who's this?"

"A friend. He lives here."

The cop mused on this and said, "Never seen you before."

"I swim mostly in the East River, by the fireboat."

"That's why," the cop said. Then, turning to the filly, he said, "What you doing later, Red?"

"Later than when?" she asked.

"Okay," the cop said. "I get it. See you around."

They walked. Red said, "You seem to have trouble dragging that leg. Wanna sit down a minute?"

They did, on a slatted bench still wet from the rain. After a while, he said, "I'm a dull man. I'm a very dull one."

"That's true," she said. "And colorless."

"I always wanted to be colorless and not bother anyone."

"Well, you don't bother me!" she said, in a voice that cheered him, just as the rain began to turn to snow.

"I used," he said, "to love to read about famous horses. That's how I came to like them. Like the Lone Ranger's horse, Silver, or King Alexander's horse, Bucephalus, or Quixote's horse, Rocinante."

"I don't read much," she said. "I'm not for the life of the mind, like Aloysius or Jake, who's always reading—and I don't mean for the odds."

"I never knew that horses liked to read."

"That's sad. Sad that you don't know a thing!"

He was afraid he had hurt her feelings, his not knowing this about horses, so he said, "I always wanted a life without misfortune. So it's been a life without much range."

She said nothing. He the same. The snow fell on them and around them and whitened the black branches of the naked trees and the black tops of the park's iron railings. Red said, "I always like the snow and the way it tells us new things."

"I like the way it makes everything quiet for a while," Louis said, wanting to add to the conversation.

It was darkening, the snow deepening and swirling like little white tornadoes.

"It's getting cold now. I'm going back to the bar," she said. "I can enjoy the snow through the window."

He was cold but didn't want to leave. He didn't want to go home. The stairs, the climb, dragging his leg, the same door, the same key, the same turning on the hall light, the same 125 watts.

"I'll walk you back, if you like," Louis said.

"Don't you have a cane?" Red asked.

He did, but he had left his house without it, not wanting to seem old.

"I have three for decoration but forgot them at home."

"Well then, get ahold of me, 'cause I don't want you to slip and fall."

The pathway was heaping up with snow and the tree

branches bent under its wet weight. He could hear the rumble of the snow trucks sent out to do their work, and the cries of the snowball fighters far down Avenue B. They walked cautiously, he gripping the snow-topped park rail until his hand went numb.

Red stopped. "Louis, why don't you climb aboard and I'll give you a ride home. Then I can walk back to the bar myself."

"Not possible. I never let a lady walk alone at night." It was not true, but he felt heroic saying this and he wanted her to feel his heroism.

She shook off the snow in gentle, slow sways. He brushed away the little white ridge left on her head and spine.

"I could come to your place," Red said carefully, "but I suppose you don't have an elevator."

Louis imagined her standing in his living room, her hooves leaving little puddles of snow, making the fading roses on the carpet bloom, the steam from her body and breath painting the walls with tropical color.

"No elevator," he said, "but maybe now I'll move where there is one."

They heard a voice through the snow.

"Hey, Red, wondering if you lost your way in this blizzard." It was the police horse.

Then, seeing Louis, he said, "Still here, chum?"

"Thanks for looking after me," Red said. "But we're copacetic."

The horse said, "Oh! Sure, Red," and wedged himself between the filly and the man, shouldering him against the rail and slowly pressing the wind out of him.

"Don't be a jerk, Harry. Stop! Or you'll never see me again."

"Come on, it's just a friendly shove," the police horse said.

"Lay off, or I'll get you eighty-sixed from the bar forever."

Harry stopped and in a small, childish voice said, "I'm sorry, Red, and you, too, mister."

He backed away into the curtaining snow and darkness and called out from a distance, "I'm not sorry at all."

"Louis, you don't look so good," Red said.

His ribs hurt and he spoke with a wheeze. "I'm all right, Red, I just need to catch my wind."

They stood for a moment, he wavering against her, while the snow tumbled down on them in clumps.

"I think you should come back to the bar, Louis. You're going blue. You could use a drink," she said.

"Sure, Red, let's go, then." Louis gave her his bravest smile.

They slowly made their way to the bar, where Aloysius greeted them and Jake said, "Back from the South Pole already?"

"Aloysius, let's fix up Louis here with a drink. Something special," Red said. "He's going soft under the gills."

They sat at the table; Louis sank weakly in the chair. Jake said, "He's all wet and going green."

The bartender thought about it and said, "I have something here, something very old, from the days when the Greeks fermented their wine with grapes from a sacred mountain grove, grapes that sucked iron power from the sun."

"That mountain," Jake said, "where Plato threw dice with the gods."

"Oh! That wild man in love with horses," Patch said. "Did he ever know we horses dreamed him his ideas?"

"We read and we write and we dream. We dream the books that all the books in the world come from. We dreamed books before the Earth got cool. We dreamed books before the invention of Time," Jake said.

Sally, her head on the bar counter, looked up and said in a sloppy voice, "It's always life in the past you talk about, but where are we now, tell me?"

Then she gave a long look over to the table and said, "Hello, Mr. Banker, buy a lady a drink?"

"Yes," Louis said.

"Bring me the best," Sally said to the bartender, but then she put her head back on the counter and fell asleep.

"It's hard not being young and a star of the ring," Red said. "You didn't have to buy her a drink, but it was sweet of you."

"You know," Jake said, "now I see that you don't look like a fish of any kind at all."

"Like a beached whale?" Louis asked. "Like a whale in the snow?"

"No, not at all," Patch said.

"You look like something in the becoming," Jake said, tilting his head.

Aloysius brought over a golden drink glowing with the drowned light of an old sun.

Louis sipped until color came back to his face. "Feeling better," he said, but then he shivered in the cold of his wet clothes.

"You should go home and get into bed," Red said, "before you catch the pneumonia."

"Oh! Not right now," the man said, his cheeks flushed. "I like it here, my friends," he said, raising his glass.

Aloysius went to the door and opened it to a wall of mounting snow. A wind of flakes swarmed through the room.

"Sorry, but I doubt if you can leave now anyway," he said to Louis. "You can't walk in these drifts, and there's nothing moving in sight."

"Wonderful, I'll stay awhile, I'll stay till spring," Louis said.

"You can stay the night," Aloysius said, "just as long as you don't have another drop."

"He's not drunk," Red said. "He's pleased."

"Not drunk at all," Louis said, rising, glass in hand.

"I drink to you all and to this retreat, to this cave, to this glade of dreamers. I drink to becoming."

"He's feverish," Jake said, "his face is sending off sparks."

"It's hot in here," Louis said, "even though I'm freezing."

Aloysius and Red led him to a back room with three stalls of hay. Louis undressed to his shorts and stretched himself out in the straw.

"Take this," Aloysius said, covering him with a thick horse blanket. And turning to Red, the bartender said, "I think we're all glued here till morning."

"Don't use that word, it gives me the chills," Red said.

"What's the difference," Aloysius said, "the glue or the ashes? The soul is immortal."

"I always wondered," Louis said, suddenly raising his head.

He could not sleep and wished they would return, all of them, and talk about the immortality of the soul, how the body died but the soul went on its way—to where? The straw smelled of spring and sun, and the blanket of the thick steam of horses. The streetlamp shone faintly through the window, glazing the room silver. He thought of the woman whom he had waited for and was glad she had not come. She had not made him happy and would never make him happy. He had never before been happy.

He closed his eyes and felt himself happy. And he soon slid into sleep. He was on a snow-tipped mountain in a glade surrounded by snow. The sun warmed the glade but left the mountain frozen in snow and ice. Horses grazed and drank from a pure stream. Some had wings. Some spoke nervously about the world below the mountain and of the dangers waiting there. But others said they never intended to leave the glen and did not care for the world below and for those foolish enough to have gone there. The young ones pranced and splashed in the stream and nipped at one another in amorous play but no one minded and let them be. Some horses came to speak to him. They wanted to know—as he had lived below and had visited among them—his thoughts of the world. Was the visible world the terminal end or the edge of another, invisible world? they asked. He did not know, he said. They laughed in a friendly way. And then asked: Was his body the edge of his world or just a perishable form of an invisible self that had no boundaries in time and space, that had no beginning and no end? He said he did not know, but he added that he was indifferent to the answer, happy as he now was among them in the glade. He was wise, they said. He was not sure if they were just being polite. A great golden horse with golden wings circled them, saying nothing. But then he came close, and, bending low for Louis to mount, he said, "Come, join me, if you will."

"Yes," he said, "I gladly will." They rose above the glen and flew high above the world, until it shrank into a speck among specks, and then they sped away toward the sun.

Louis woke to the clatter of life and voices in the bar and quickly dressed; his clothes were dry. All the horses of the previous evening surrounded a table heaped with buckets of grain and bowls of water. They had set aside a place for him with a plate of cooked oatmeal and a napkin and wooden spoon.

He nodded; they did the same. Then, silently, they all began to eat as the first true light of day came through the window.

The Bar at Twilight

He walked into the bar, twilight at his heels, and without thinking ordered a scotch, neat. He surveyed the room and its vacant tables. He was glad there was no TV, no music, blasting or otherwise. No colored lights brightened the liquor shelves or gave hope to the dim mirror. Nothing was there wishing to appeal, to please, nothing of false cheer and hollow welcome. But he had left his home hoping to find a bar to lift up his spirits and this was not it.

He considered making a quick exit and saying to the bartender, "Sorry, I forgot something at home." Then he'd leave a dollar—maybe even two—on the counter to show his goodwill, and skedaddle before he got further dispirited by the surroundings. Ghostly photographs of horses covering a wall had already sunk his spirits.

The bartender: She was neither tall nor short, neither blond nor brunette, neither young nor old, neither composed nor disheveled, neither enticing nor repellent, neither extraordinary nor commonplace. He soon quit trying to place her.

But before he could turn to leave, she said, "I have a single-malt scotch for you. Been mellowed in stout oak barrels for fifty years in the depths of a Highland castle, lulled to sleep at bedtime by the bagpipe's lullaby, and woken by a soft drumroll at dawn."

She poured him a shot.

He took a sip, out of courtesy. Then another. He looked around the room, which now appeared like a misty glen with a salmon-crowded brook running through it. Finally, he said, "This is the most extraordinary scotch I have ever had."

"Thought it would suit you. I spotted you for a person of distinction the moment you walked in."

"How so?"

"The artful tilt of your homburg gave you away."

"It was the blind wind that engineered that maneuver."

"The wind's a savvy artist," she said, giving the bar a towel wipe for emphasis.

A young centaur pushed through the door and spun once about the room.

"Is this the bar for horses, or have I come to the wrong place?"

"Once was," Marie said, "but they've gone."

"Gone where?" the centaur asked.

"Wherever they go when they want to go."

"My mother spoke about this place many times before she died."

"Maybe there's a picture of her on the wall," Marie said, "if she was a regular."

"May I have another?" the man asked. "A double?"

Marie half-filled a water glass. Studying it, the man said, "That's more like a quadruple."

"It was the tilt of your hat and that you said 'may' instead of 'can,' that's what distinguished you. The drink's on the house. And I'm the house."

She crossed to the other end of the bar, where a ruddy-nosed man with a sailor's watch cap and graying beard was resting his elbows on the counter. "Marie," he said, "let's go out again."

"That didn't work well the first time around."

"Didn't we have fun?"

"I liked the tugboat ride down to the Narrows. I liked your effort with the liverwurst with onion sandwiches and the cold beer and the side of dill pickles you plucked with your fingers from the jar. I even somewhat like you, Harry, even though your beard smells like wet nails."

"So? Where did I go wrong?"

"You're too old for me. Though I don't know if that's the whole of it. Who knows the whole of it anyway?"

"Not too old to love you with feeling. Profound feeling. Feeling that comes with having walked around the block a few hundred times in all weather and sailed many seas in storms and in swells the height of tall buildings, and having come to port, I now know what's to be treasured in life. I know who's an authentic woman, know how to appreciate her."

"Too old, dear Harry. Too much brine in your blood."

"What, Marie, has age to do with the heart's disposition? With its fickle waywardness and adamant devotions, with its reckless longings and childishness?"

"Anyway, Harry, I have enough in my life what with the bar, and with Red."

"Sure, Marie, but can't I fill in when Red's away?"

Outside, in Tompkins Square Park, the wind tortured the trees, wrenching leaves from their branches and speeding them into the bar's large plate-glass windows. The door rattled; dust and pigeon feathers whirled under its sill and introduced the street's chill of impending night into the warm room.

"Another storm," Marie said.

"My mother told me there were stalls for the horses in the back and that sometimes she'd sleep over if she had gotten too tipsy to trot home."

"They're stockrooms now, but they still smell of the horses' sweat and the aroma of their beer swilling," Marie said. "Sweat and piss, I mean, and their droppings, which harden into plates of straw that you step on for good luck. I miss the horses. I wish they were back."

"This is an odd place," the man said, waving his hand as if delineating the territory. "Its lack of charm is its very charm."

"You're a good example of that yourself, mister," Marie said.

"The name's Louis. Like 'Meet me in St. Louis, Louis.' Thank you for the compliment and for its brevity. In art and in life, less is more," he said, his faced flushed, his glass raised in a toast, indefinite to whom addressed.

"Not necessarily," the centaur said. "Sometimes less is simply less or sometimes less is a form of emotional stinginess, a miserliness of spirit in the guise of an aesthetic ideal."

"It's about seeking perfection, I suppose, about making things so lean that nothing may be added or subtracted," Louis said. "But the removal of all unnecessary ornamentation from a person or an object or a text or a musical note must be done with restraint and with care not to obliterate the blood and tissue and guts of the thing."

"Must never remove the stink of life from life," the centaur said. "We centaurs have known that from the beginning of time. Even though our heads and thoughts are high up to the dreamy stars, our rears, which do the shitting and pissing and copulating, keep us grounded from floating to the abstract heights."

"I would say the same," Louis said, addressing all around. "After all, I'm no delicate reed with a scented hankie stuck to his nose in the subway at rush hour. I praise the unkempt and the irrelevant, the loose ends and the unresolved, the untidy and imperfect, the ragged edges and pieces that don't fit—the incomplete, even. I praise art that sweats life and life that sweats art."

"You sure let out a lot of line, mister," Harry said. "Lots of bilge mixed with sweet water, if you don't mind my saying."

"Bilge and sweet water, isn't that life's formula, Harry?" Marie said. Addressing the world in the bar and the world beyond its door, Marie said, "When you were young, when you were just unformed things in grades just above kindergarten, did you paste dead leaves in your scrapbook? Did you one day open a trunk and find your long-forgotten scrapbook and study the dried leaves you had embalmed there, and did you say to yourself, 'Oh, look!'?"

"My mother was in love with the man she met at this bar," the centaur said. "He was the love of her very intense life."

"Was she called Red?" Marie asked, coming from behind the bar and taking a stool between the centaur and Louis.

"Yes, that was her moniker," the centaur answered. "She was in love until her last long breath."

"The love between a horse and a man is a difficult one, I imagine," Louis said. "Both physical and emotional, I'm sure."

"It posed problems, but then, what in life doesn't?" the centaur noted, raising a thick eyebrow for effect.

"The centaur makes sense, Marie. Nothing matters

when you are in love," Harry said in the voice of his fourth rye and two beer chasers. "Is that not so?"

"If you are in love," Marie replied.

"Less is more," the centaur said, "in love, too. The less of whatever clutters love, the less fat of the everyday that smothers the passion and purity of its flame is what I mean. The physical self is nothing but a caretaker of that flame, and the flame burns in the souls of lovers, horse or man, young or old, even after death."

"Only the very rich can love so totally," Marie said, "unencumbered, as they are, by what you call the 'fat of the everyday.' Only the rich or those who can love purely, unrequitedly. As I love this bar, for example."

"Are you more horse or more man?" Louis asked the centaur.

"In equal distribution," the centaur said. "Neither predominates, but the blend of both has made me—made my kind—rather special. We can, for example, discern patterns in the stars."

"And your father?" Marie asked. "Of what stuff was he made?"

"The stuff of humans who were lonely and through love became less lonely."

"These are the consolations of love, Marie," Harry said in the bleary voice of his fifth rye. "Consolations both temporal and eternal."

"My father was an ordinary man, an ordinary clerk in an ordinary midtown office," the centaur continued.

"He lived alone across the park from here on Tenth. He knew little of life except for his desk in the day and dinner at a local Polish restaurant after work—mushroom soup, black bread, and a vodka, neat—his daily fare. He was a sweet, solitary man and would have lived and died alone until he accidentally wandered into this very bar, and met my mother, the recently retired circus show horse."

"Marie, let's tug downriver to the Narrows and this time we'll make for the open sea and out into the vast itself, out and beyond until we blend with the sky."

"I'm a landlocked woman, Harry. I like the firm ground underfoot. I love the elms and paths winding through the park."

A tug's long hoot from the East River caressed the bar, leaving all there in a mood of ineffable longing.

The centaur grew melancholy and said, "There are times when one must go home, or to its nearest facsimile. I think I'm going home."

Louis said, "There are moments too sad for anything but compassionate oblivion."

Harry said, "I wish I had a dog that didn't bark or shit or shed or smell bad with a bad wet stink after a walk in the rain. I wish I had that kind of dog."

"There is nothing like the mournful call of a tug to summon up thoughts of love and death and what lies in the between," Marie said, sinking a double shot of scotch and pulling a face between pleasure and pain.

The snow rushed the night sky and clotted the

windows with an icy silver sheen that spread over the bar and its inhabitants.

"Look at us," the centaur said. "We're like ghosts with sheets."

"Marie, I'd be happy to be a ghost if I could be a ghost with you," Harry said.

"A ghost in love," Louis said. "There's something in that to suggest that death might be worth living for. By the way, Miss Marie, isn't that a piano in the back?" he asked, nodding to the gloom at the end of the corridor. The drink had warmed him, puffed up his spirits.

"A piano from the horse-bar days," Marie said. "Never played since."

"Mind if I try it?"

"Only if you don't murder the air with sugary sonatas or bubbly waltz melodies."

Louis dusted the keys with his handkerchief and gave his wrists a few twirls and cracked his fingers and gave them a few warming rubs before hitting the keys, which produced notes like milk gone sour. The centaur reared and whinnied: "Stop, please! It's killing my will to live."

"You call that music?" Harry said. "Stop fooling around."

"Give him a chance," Marie said. "He's just warming up to it."

"May I continue, then?" Louis asked.

He began with an assortment of melodies by Chopin, and just as the air was enjoying the romantic mood of moonlight and champagne, he switched to some jazzy sketches that hinted at store-bought bourbon and hand-rolled cigarettes in a brothel on lower Maple Street in the New Orleans of the twenties.

But soon Louis dived into his innermost core, producing music keyed to a tug's mournful hoot and to the swoosh of its wide wake and to the tones of an owl preaching in a cemetery at midnight and to the wild cries of the river gulls.

The piano trembled, seeing the cold East River gazing up at the Brooklyn and Manhattan Bridges, waiting for the next jumper; nights spent in a furnished room with a forty-watt bulb dangling from a crack in the ceiling; a dying cat shivering in a patch of moonlight on the windowsill; the soul's darkness at the basement of the heart; the first shovelful of earth on the coffin of the woman you love.

"He makes joy of the Futile and the Why-Go-On? He makes perfume from bouquets rotting at the roadside. He tells Death to fuck off. He shames Death's jealousy of Life. He makes Death long for a day off. He makes Death yearn to make love. He plucks Beauty from Death," Marie said.

"Yes, yes, Miss Marie, even his pauses between notes open to eternity and to the moment after," the centaur noted, his head bowed.

Louis had earlier, in the day's shadow, left his apartment overlooking Tompkins Square Park, having chosen, from all the others on his rack, a homburg. He left behind a sailor's cap; a sombrero he'd bought in Chapingo, Mexico; a cowboy hat from Fort Worth, Texas; and a brand-new beret found on a bench in Barcelona. The snow would ruin the homburg, take years from its youth, fade it before its time, drain out its original ivory-black color, and coarsen its supple skin. But he wanted to stroll about with a jaunty hat, to appear jaunty, debonair, pleased with himself, even, as if life and he were on good terms.

He would look, before the light had failed, for a café to buoy him up, a place with attractive people with attractive lives, and conversation to match, a place that was somewhere close by so he could easily walk home should the snow pile up to the sky and barricade the streets and make a glacier of the park and its pathways. As it was, snow was mounting the park, topping the black iron railings with crumbly white lines; sparrows fell from the trees and buried themselves in the white; Jason, the hawk, swooped down from the Christodora building on the park side of Avenue B and snatched a snow-coated rat feasting from a spilled-over trash can. A shivering old woman wrapped in newspapers slept on a park bench, the snow blanketing her with a soft coat to warm her dying.

Maybe a woman at the café would glean that he was a good sort, lonely but not desperate; maybe she would see from his eyes that he was on the sincere side, that he was vulnerable, intelligent, courteous, kind, brave, even. Maybe she would see that he had a feel for style but was not driven by it, that he understood style's place in the discourse of everyday life, that one could be rightly or wrongly measured by it, to be seen to have or have not made an effort to brighten the lackluster day and to give life a little push toward the sun.

Maybe there would be a woman there who could don the comic mask when needed, a face to keep up her spirits—and of those in her circle—and profess the charm of life, the ever-lively fun of it, so that neither she nor those whose company she graced ever saw in her a troubled, brooding, crushed moment. Never would anyone see her wear her true, tragic mask, and her need to seek comfort in the East River, in its depths, all the way to the bottom, among discarded rubber tires, strangled babies, and murdered cats, all the way down to its soulless muck.

"You play like a revelation, like the first green buds of spring, like the death rattle that sounds the end and the beginning. You play like everything that can't be said in words. Play us another," Marie asked when Louis had struck his last note and rose, pale, from the piano.

Pale, as if he had learned of the suicide of a woman he loved. As if the woman he loved had walked out his door to spread open her thighs to another man in his thousand-ply Egyptian cotton sheets in the tonier reaches of Park Avenue, with twenty-four-hour doormen and a private spot in the basement garage. And maybe even with a fully equipped gym and a lap pool on the roof, *en plus.* As if he had just been told his blood was swimming with cancer, which was tirelessly doing laps in his bloodstream. Cancer drunk on blood, and taking little bites here and there, a nibble of liver, a snippet of pancreas, a morsel of kidney, never stopping, multiplying like fucking rabbits, like fucking drunk amoebas.

"I've reached my limit for now," Louis said, "but I may revive presently, depending on the disposition of the weather, depending on the developing cut of the company, depending on whether I can wipe clean the memory slate and leave fixed there nothing but void. Depending on the next drink, which I hope will be as exhilarating as the last."

Twilight finally surrendered and tumbled into black night. Snow shrouded the windows, turning the bar into a dim cave without shadows.

"Marie, we need more light in here," Harry said. "I can't see beyond my nose in this two-bit obscurity. We need brighter bulbs, bulbs whose light stretches to the limits of the room and pours out the window and pools into the street. Light that cheers the heart and plucks it from ruminations on the inequity of unrequited love and other such disquieting *pensées.*"

"Quite elegantly put, Harry," Marie said. "I need a stroll. My heart's pounding with Louis's music. Pounding in a ravishing way, that is, Louis. *Tu vois?*"

"I'll go with you," Harry said. "Let's go down to the river and watch it congeal and freeze itself into ice."

"The weather may be an impediment to your

excursion, Mr. Harry, but why don't we all take a peep outside, to be sure," the centaur said.

"Good idea," Harry said.

"Why not?" Louis said.

"What are we waiting for?" Marie said.

The four huddled together, shivering on the sidewalk. They searched the impenetrable sky for a sign of its clearing, and could not bring themselves to move even as the snow climbed their bare heads.

"I can't see my hand," Marie said.

"I can't see my shoe," Louis said.

"I can't see your face, Marie. Come closer!" Harry said.

A sudden opening in the sky cleared a way to the stars while the snow continued to fall.

"Look up now," the centaur said. "There's Orion and his diamond belt, and there are the Big and Little Dippers—signifying nothing but direction for mariners and desert nomads. But here, in that cluster of stars north of Venus, much is said."

"Do they say my tug will leave the slip with Marie as my first and only mate?" Harry asked.

"Do they say that the soul is immortal?" Louis asked.

"Do they say that a woman may be won by the unexpected? By the surprise of a man's smile as he turns when you call his name? Does it say when my Red will come home?" Marie asked.

"The stars do not answer inquiries or predict outcomes," the centaur said. "They forewarn of disasters weatherwise and otherwise, and sometimes they tell character."

Snow walled the deserted streets and buried the cars. Snow shrouded the park and its trees, filling in even the empty spaces between the branches. Snow converted the benches into white catafalques and the park into a silhouette of trees and statues, obliterating entirely the iron railings. Snow trucks rumbled their engines in the distance, from maybe as far away as Avenue D, where they had massed to attack the mounting whiteness but remained idling, unable to move a foot. Tugs, locked fast in the crushing ice of the East River, shrieked like foxes in the hunter's trap. Ships and boats large and small struggled to make their escape, their propellers futilely grinding the ice that healed itself in place.

The four began their retreat to the bar, but the snow had climbed so high that they had to burrow through in single file, the centaur at the lead, plowing ahead with his broad chest. When they finally got inside, they stood mute, blue in the face, their teeth chattering, even the centaur's, until Harry said, "Marie, haul out the good stuff. This is the time for it if ever there was."

"White noise, white nights, white heat, white marriage, white lies, white coffee, white waters, white whales, white flags, whiteout," Louis said, trying to unlock his frozen jaw.

"I once," Marie said, "peered into a highland cave in Peru. It was pure blackness, absent of sound and vacant of light. I saw then what extinction was made of, the final oblivion of the self. Except, I thought, what if after my death I were to become an atom, an atom with memory and consciousness speeding through eternity and unable to speak, to communicate, unable to love. So, whiteness comforts me—I sleep on a white bed with white pillows and wool blankets whiter than white."

Marie said this as she drew a bottle from under the bar, a bottle that glowed with the fire of an ancient Mediterranean sun, sending its warm golden rays throughout the room.

"The horses left me this bottle," Marie said, "left it to me as their memento, and with the wish that I treat this bar with tenderness for the lost and the sad."

"It should be packed, then," Louis said, "packed day and night."

"It's a mystery how only a few find this place, though it is clearly visible, and how few enter only a few steps beyond the doorway before they turn about," Marie said. "As you were about to do, Louis. And, as for the young who swarm this neighborhood, the young who have eyes only for the young, they pass by, not seeing what's through the window, but seeing only reflections of themselves."

"Let's drink to the snow that keeps us here. Let's drink," Harry said, "to the expectations of love that keep hope alive."

They drank and soon their faces returned to the

various shades natural to each. The snow melted away from them, pooling silver puddles at their feet. They looked about and up and down and sideways and wondered at life. "Life, life, life," Louis intoned.

"Is there anything more grand?" Harry asked the corrugated tin ceiling from 1903, when horses had first made the bar theirs.

"Nothing," the centaur said, raising a hoof, his left one.

"I'll bet my life on life, anytime," Marie said, hoisting the glass of glowing amber she swirled into a baby whirlpool.

"I feel," the centaur said, "that the clocks have vanished and there is neither past nor future, but a calm eternal present and that we are the last persons alive, that the world has perished in the snow."

"Yes," Louis said. "Perished in the snow and taken all the memory of the world with it."

"Let's drink to the vanished world," Marie said.

"To us," Louis said.

"To insatiable dreams and fair winds," Harry said.

"To this bar and all breathing in it," Marie said.

The centaur rose on his hind legs, staying aloft for some moments before returning to land, where, once again firmly planted, he said, "Let's drink to my ancestors who walked among sex-drunk satyrs in lush mountain glades, where baby grapes bulged with longing for the sun, to my ancestors who swam among river gods and river nymphs, who sang to them. Let's drink to my ancestors who were philosophers before philosophy and, being beast and human, had the wisdom of both."

"That's a sweet toast," Harry said. "But what's philosophy compared to love that needs no philosophy?"

"We've come a long way from those golden times you speak of, centaur, if, indeed, those times ever existed," Louis said. "We imagine the past as always better than the present. But it was never better except in our wishes, in our soothing tales of make-believe. My earliest ancestors lived in freezing caves and dreaded every uncertain moment of the day. They feared the moonless black night even more—feared that some beast or fellow human might steal into their icy den and gut them in their sleep. For them, moon or no, it was always night! The sun was only on loan. They clubbed and ate one another for food and power, but they also painted scenes of animals on their cave walls, and in that effort to make art we see in our brutish ancestors our common and highest humanity."

"We lived, but we made no record. All of our records were drawn and written by others, by the mythmakers. And now there are only three of us remaining, and soon we shall be none," the centaur said.

"How sad," Marie said. "But you are with us now, centaur."

"I have a distant cousin who lives in Queens, but she's a misanthrope and a shut-in and is tired of life anyway.

And there's another cousin who lives in hiding in Greece, fearful of being hunted down and exhibited in a cage."

"Bring him here to live with us," Marie said.

"I don't think so. He lives in the high mountains and loves cold streams and swaying pines. In any case," the centaur continued, "I forgot to mention that the stars have sent us greetings. They suggested we stay safely within the bar because the blizzard will worsen and danger awaits us out there in the drifts."

"Let's take a chance anyway, Marie, and go down to the river," Harry said. "Let's go down to the river and see the ice floes and hold hands like kids in love."

"I've sailed many rivers," Louis said. "I've rafted on the Ganges and seen on its banks the dead burn away on skimpy funeral pyres, seen their crumbly ashes strewn in the river's moody flow, and I understood that finally we were only in transit to ashes, and that after death nothing in the beyond waits for us. All our memories, too, gone up in smoke and scattered in the ashes, just some bits of ash to show for what was a life. What an affront! Needless to say, I do not love the Ganges."

"What a Gloomy Gus you are," Harry said.

"I have lived on a houseboat on the Seine," Louis continued, "the Louvre at my back, Notre-Dame in my window, swans pecking at my hull for attention; known the river's swanky rhythm, its swells and splash, and felt its claims to historical stature. Yet, I do not love the Seine. Or the Tiber, the Amazon, or the Rhine or the

Thames, or the Hudson or that silted stream they call the mighty Mississippi."

"Yes," Harry said. "But the East River! The stark East River, which flows without decoration or embellishments, without froufrou, without anything but boats and ships and tankers and tugs, or an occasional sail or skiff on a lark, that's my kind of river. Let's go down there, Marie, and let's burn the ice on a sweet green bench."

"Hope Red's okay. Hope he's not stuck in the snow."

"To die in the snow. That's an elegant way to die," the centaur said. "Peaceful, I'm told. Many of my horse ancestors died that way on the retreat from Moscow, where Napoléon's cavalry froze en masse in the snow, horse and rider still standing and stuck fast in the ice that encased them. Ice statues on an ice plinth, they were. A noble death for both horse and rider, I would say."

Snow divided the window, half snow, half sky, a glacier pressing against the window, envious of the life behind it.

"Is there more of this elixir?" Louis asked, laying a twenty on the bar, and Marie replied, not sharply but with a significant edge, "Yes, but not for money. Certainly not for money."

"For love, then," Louis said.

"There's the dream," Marie said.

"The word *dream* and the snow crushing against the window set me to thinking about a young man I knew of," Louis said. "A German lad en route to an engineering career, but, on discovering he had tuberculosis, he went to be cured in a clinic high in the Swiss Alps, where he remained for seven years. For pleasure, and to break from the daily routine of his cure, he, one late afternoon, hiked high above the snow line and found himself caught in a sudden blizzard. He took shelter in a kind of broken-down, doorless shed that left him exposed to the snow and the freezing cold. The blizzard was so thick that he could not see two feet beyond him, and he was unable to tell up from down and east from west or get any directional hint of how to find his way back to the clinic. He did not know if he had been in the shed for hours or for days or years or from the moment he was born. He drifted in a sweet delirium of timeless time.

"He lay down and closed his eyes and grew drowsy, dreamy, increasingly sleepy as the afternoon grew into night, but, knowing the deathly consequences, he fought sleep. But he also thought how easy and how pleasant it would be to surrender joyfully to Morpheus and let himself freeze to death in the sleepy god's comforting embrace.

"I, too," Louis continued, "had started out the afternoon seeking a place to distract me from myself, finding instead a place that has invited me to die in company."

"Touch my forehead, Marie—careful, don't scorch your fingers. I'm burning like a crazy furnace, burning for want of you," Harry said.

"I don't ever remember having as much fun as this,"

the centaur said. "Or ever meeting people like you. Or centaurs like me. May I say, Mr. Harry, that I wish one day to love as powerfully as you do this woman here."

"You may call me Marie, centaur."

Marie disappeared into the kitchen behind the bar and soon returned with a tray that she placed on the table directly under the snow-crowded window. She set down, in this order, a plate of sliced onions, curled at the edges; a chipped plate of seven unsliced Polish pickles; a bowl of saltine crackers, some crumbled; a plate of yellowish cheese, rubbery in texture; a shot glass packed with toothpicks in see-through cellophane envelopes; a plate of twelve anemic sausages that were on the way to death in the fridge and were glad for the reprieve; and a four-inch hunk of liverwurst.

"Hands off the liverwurst," Marie said. "That's on hold."

From nowhere, she produced a bottle of greenish Polish vodka, Żubrówka, and with casual authority stuck it into a crystal bucket of crushed ice. And, from the same nowhere, she topped the table with a single red rose in a Lalique vase and two handcrafted beeswax candles—or maybe it was goose wax—in eighteenth-century English silver holders with their time-accrued gray patina, giving them a historical flair. Or maybe the holders were Regency and not Georgian. Maybe they were French, even, and ransacked from the home of guillotined aristocrats.

"*À table, tout le monde.* Let's feast, let's banquet, let's chow down, let's dig in, gents," Marie said.

"It is very difficult—indeed, physically impossible—for me to sit as you all do. Excuse me if I remain standing," the centaur said. "And forgive me, too, should I dampen your spirits, but I do not eat meat or other things that live on land or sea or range the skies."

"You, centaur, are a gentleman," Harry said. "Your courtesy sets an example for me. I apologize to all for my earlier embarrassing amatory outbursts, however passionately and earnestly inspired."

"Merci, Monsieur Harry. *Vous parlez du coeur. Vous avez toute ma sympathie. Et mon amitié,*" the centaur said, speaking in a language alien to him and that he had never before employed.

Soon, they were all speaking in French. And gesturing in French with shoulder shrugs to indicate their indifference to fate and twisting their cheeks to show their pleasure with this or that morsel or sip. The translation follows:

"This meal well pleases me," Louis said.

"I wish my mother had set the table and served her meals with such organized refinement," Harry said. "Perhaps it would have shown me the way to a higher life, one with delicacy of expression rather than what has molded me into the coarse man you see here."

"I do not find you coarse, dear Harry. On the contrary," Louis said, "your very concern that you might be woven of rough stuff proves otherwise, and reveals a sensitive nature beneath your guise of a rough old sea salt."

"I served her pickles in a jar and a liverwurst sandwich. I see now what did me in."

"Don't make too much of it on that score, Harry," Marie said. "You were thoughtful enough to cut in some freshly sliced onions."

"One eats well here. Moreover, and more importantly, the rose touches me," the centaur said. "Its significant form arouses the instinct for the beautiful and the elevated, and its fragility reminds us of the evanescent nature of life and that even the beautiful die, is it not so?"

"Thank you all," Marie said, "for piercing through the facade of my unadorned presentation to fathom the core of its aesthetic—and may I say, existential—program. 'Less is more,' as someone opined earlier, at some simpler time when the world was not fastened in snow and sunk in night, when we were young and passionate for truth, when we'd rather have been right than happy, when we thought happiness was waiting for us just around the corner and when we never imagined our hearts splintered and set in a cast of ice-cream sticks and rubber bands, when we never thought that we would be, out of the air, speaking French and, in that tongue, sense our mutual affection."

Louis felt a breeze, a turbulence of plates. A strong cat had leapt to the table and, uninvited, was on the liverwurst, tongue first, with little raspy licks.

Marie, returning to English, said, "Oh! Red, dear, you've come home."

The cat gave her an acknowledging nod before dragging the prize onto the sawdust floor, where he chewed away with the manic gusto of the starved.

"I had a cat once," Louis said. "Nicolino."

"Did he run away?" the centaur asked.

"Did he get married and go off with his bride, and live with his rich in-laws in the suburbs?" Harry asked.

"Did he die?" Marie asked.

"Died of grief," Louis said. "Of grief."

The cat ate until only a little mound of the liverwurst was left. He waddled to a corner of the bar, spun about three times before gagging, and, finally, vomited up a ball of meat and fur.

"He'll go away and hide until I clean it up," Marie said. "He knows I always will. I was born to clean up another's mess, as long as it's a cat's."

"The stars indicated that about you," the centaur said. "They were very clear about it tonight."

"Died from the poison that was meant for the rats who rule this park he so loved to prowl," Louis said. "I left the fire escape window open to him in all weather and he came and went as he chose. One morning, I got a call from a parkie who'd found him and had read his name tag with my phone number. He had the humanity to ask if I wanted to come collect Nicolino's little corpse, or otherwise he would dispose of it in the usual way."

"What way was that?" Marie asked.

"First the dumpster," Louis said, "and then carted off to the grinder and ground. Nicolino had been grieving over a svelte Persian who had left him for a pedigreed tom from First and Seventh. In no time, she squeezed out a litter of eight on a kilim rug. I saw Nicolino slowly pine away and drag himself from room to room and sulk at the window and crawl down the fire escape, his head lowered like that of a defeated man. Well, after all, he was defeated. Grief had drained his soul and the rat poison finished him."

"There are so many tales of love. I read dozens of them on my long sea passages," Harry said, "and I learned that the best is to end before the eventual boredom, recriminations, and contempt."

"As I was saying," Louis said, "the young German felt himself easing into a painless, welcoming death. Haven't you at a lecture or at a sermon longed to close your eyes and had to fight with all your might to keep them open? Open, so as not to be publicly disgraced or to disgrace your companion beside you, and haven't you thought at that moment it was better to die than to hear another word?

"Imagine, then, this young man's wish to surrender his life. What did another hour or day matter when it would be over anyway, sooner or later, one time or another? In fact, better now when it was so comfortable to die in the soft snow and in the softening night and call it quits. What was ahead for him anyway? Some moments of pleasure, the fleeting ecstasy of music, and maybe a few seconds of joy seeing a hawk in flight, the orgasm, the early days of love? The rest, at best, was the ennui of daily life; the worst, the fall into decrepitude and illness, into loneliness and loss. What was the point struggling to stay awake when it was so inviting—so delicious, in fact—to sleep in the eternal night for eternity?"

"Who is this friend? Was it you?" the centaur asked.

They stood in the tall gloom of the ever-freezing, ever-darkening bar, each sending out a sound of displeasure with his or her abject condition: a groan, a snort, a sigh, a "whew."

Until, finally, one said, "Let's ride out of here," and another, "Let's weigh anchor." Louis said nothing, but he pointed to the door and nodded three times. Finally, Marie said, "Last one out turns off the lights."

"You may have noticed," the centaur said, "that the power and the lights have been out for some while and the candles themselves are inching toward extinction."

❖

Who first said "Let's go?" Who fetched the smelly horse blankets left moldering in the old stalls? Who first pulled open the ice-trimmed door to the icy night? Who took the tenuous first steps into the snow-piled sidewalk?

No matter: We soon were out into the white. Marie rode sidesaddle on the centaur's broad back; Red, who had appeared from some burrow in the bar, nestled himself in Marie's arms. Harry clung to the centaur's flowing tail, and I followed behind in the centaur's narrow wake. The man in the moon loomed above, casting us all in a silver glow. He was crowned with a sailor's watch cap and wore a tartan scarf about his cheesy neck. The ice had frozen his goofy smile.

We staggered our way through Avenues B, C, and D, pausing at the lightless housing projects, which loomed like giant walls of black ice to block our progress. But we soon wended our way through and crossed East River Drive, bereft of cars and persons, through the park, until we finally made it to the river, where we found tugs, oilers, and barges locked in ice. A helicopter hung, like a mosquito, in the icy membrane of the sky.

We stood at the railing and watched the ice cracking below to form a channel just wide enough for a tug to make its way and halt before us, its engine churning the water into a frothy boil before it went dead and silence encased itself in ice. Lilac sprigs rose from the tug's prow, scenting the air, the fragrance melting the jagged edges of the ice sheet that had draped itself over the tug.

The captain, preceded by billows of cherry-flavored smoke from his chunky pipe, emerged on the deck. He smiled with jack-o'-lantern teeth, and his ruddy cheeks glowed with hearty life. He was, I thought, a man who had filled his days and who loved his beef and stout and long after-dinner naps.

"Come aboard the *Arcadia*," he said in a cheery voice.

"Bound for where, are you?" Harry said, his voice half suspicion, half delight.

"We are bound for warmer climes, where there is neither sun nor moon, neither morning nor night, but an ever-mellow amber afternoon."

"Is there room for me?" the centaur asked.

"We'll fix you a cozy berth," the captain said, setting out the gangplank for us to tread.

"What do you say, Marie?" Harry asked.

"As long as Red can come along."

"Cats are loved here," the captain said.

"May I join, too, Captain?" I asked, wishing not to be parted from my friends.

"You, Louis, have been long awaited," the captain said with a welcoming wave of his pipe.

We boarded and were soon weaving downriver, the night and ice parting before us. We were soon fast upon the Narrows and I knew that in no time we would attain the open sea.

The Tower

Sometimes his urine was cloudy. Sometimes gritty with what he called "gravel." Sometimes his piss flowed bloody and frightening. No matter how disturbing, Montaigne recorded his condition in his travel journal as coolly as he did the daily weather. He was always in various degrees of pain, and he noted that, too, but dispassionately, like a scientist in a white lab coat.

Even before he suffered from kidney stones and the burning pain that came with them, Montaigne had long thought about death, and not only his own. He had thought about how to meet it and if doing so gracefully would change the encounter. His closest friend, the man he had loved more than anyone in the world, was to love more than anyone in the world, had died with calm dignity. In his last minutes, in his last words, his dear friend did not begrudge life or beg for more time or express regrets over what was left undone or make apologies to those he might have or had offended or injured. Montaigne thought that when death approached, he would neither wave him away nor welcome him, but say to death's shadow on the wall, "Finally, no more pain."

I put my book aside when she walked in.

"I'm leaving you," she said. She had a red handbag on her arm.

"For how long?"

"For always."

"And what about Pascal, will you take him?"

"He's always favored you." I was very glad. I could see Pascal sitting in the dining room doorway, pretending not to listen.

"Yes, that's true."

"Don't you care to know why I'm leaving?" she asked, petulantly, I thought.

"I suppose you'll tell me."

"I will, but maybe another time." She stared at me as if wondering who I was. Then she started to speak but was interrupted by a car-horn blast. I looked out the window and saw a taxi with a man behind the wheel.

"May I help you with your bags?" I asked.

"I'll send for them later, if you don't mind."

"Who will you send?"

"The person who comes." She stared at me another moment and then left.

I heard a motor start up, then the swerve of the car leaving the curb. Pascal took his time walking over to me and then, with a faint cry, he jumped into my lap, curling himself on my open book. I stroked his head until he made that little motor purr that all cats make when they pretend to love you.

One day, Montaigne went all the way from his home in Bordeaux to Italy for its famous physicians and for a change in diet, for that country's warm climate and healing sky. He went to soak himself in the mineral baths, which sometimes gave him relief—also noted in his journal. He recorded but never whined about the biting stones in his kidneys or the bedbugs in the mattress in a Florence hostel or complained about that city's summer heat, so great that he slept on a table pressed against an open window.

He traveled alone. Once, in Rome, Montaigne hired a translator, a fellow Frenchman, who, without notice or reason, left him without a good-bye. So, armed with maps and charts and curiosity, he went about the city with himself for company and guide. In that ancient city he witnessed horrific public executions of criminals, men drawn and quartered while still alive. He visited the libraries of cardinals and nobles, returning to his hostel to note in the same disinterested voice the books and the tortures he had seen and the hard stone that had that day passed through his urethra.

I knew there was no hope in lifting Pascal up and dropping him on the carpet so that he would leave me in peace to read. I knew he would just bound up again and sit on my book again and that he would do the same 101 times before I gave up and left the room or left the house or left the city. So I took the string with a little ball attached to it that I kept tucked under the pillow and let it drop on the floor. He leapt off my lap and began pawing the rubber ball. I pulled it away and he followed with a one-two punch. Montaigne had once asked himself, Is it I who plays with the cat or is it he who plays with me?

The house seemed full now that she had gone, the rooms packed with me. I wandered about, savoring the quiet, the solitude, the way my books, sleeping on their shelves, seemed to glow as I passed by—old friends who no longer need share me with another. I thought I would spend the rest of the day without a plan and do as I wished. Maybe I would sit all day and read. Maybe I would go out with my gun and empty the streets of all the noise. I would then at last have a silent, empty house surrounded by a tranquil, soundless zone. That was just a thought. I have no gun.

After his beloved friend died, Montaigne went into seclusion, keeping himself in a turreted stone tower at the edge of his estate. It was cold in winter and hot in summer and not well lit, the windows being small. He had had a very full life up to the point of his withdrawal, if fullness means social activity and a role in governing. He was a courtier in the royal court and the mayor of Bordeaux and was always out day and night doing things. But now in that tower, Montaigne was determined to write, which he did, essays, which some believe were addressed to his dead friend. His mind traveled everywhere, his prose keeping apace with all the distances and places his mind traveled. He wrote about cannibals. He wrote about friendship. What is friendship? he asked, and answered, When it is true, it is greater than any bond of blood. Brothers have in common the same port from whence they were issued but may be separated forever by jealousy and rivalry in matters of inheritance and property. Brothers may hate each other, kill each other, as the Old Testament so vividly illustrates. But friends choose each other and their intercourse deepens in trust, esteem, and affection; their intellectual exchange strikes flames.

He stayed in his tower for ten years, his world winnowed down to a stone room of books and a wooden table. Crows sat on his window ledge and studied him, imperturbable in their presence. His wife visited and, in his place, saw a triangle. Sometimes he would look at his friend's portrait on the table, a miniature in a plain silver frame, and say, "We've worked enough for now, let's have lunch. What do you think?" Sometimes he just stayed in place until the evening, when he dined on cold mutton and lentils and read in the wintry candlelight. Once, as he climbed the stairs to his bedchamber, he noticed his bent shadow trailing him on the wall. Just some years ago his shadow had bounded ahead of him, waiting for him to catch up. Now he grew tired easily; writing a page took hours and he was always in pain. He pissed rich blood. He howled. But he sat and wrote until he finished his book. Then he went on his extensive travels.

I went into the kitchen and made a dish of pears and Stilton and broke out the water biscuits; I opened the best wine I had ever bought, one so expensive that I had hidden it from her, waiting for the right occasion to spring it. I sat at the kitchen table. Pascal leaped up to join me. I opened a can of boneless sardines, drained the oil, slid the fish onto a large white plate, and set it beside me so that Pascal and I could lunch together. He was suspicious, sniffed, then retreated, and then returned to the same olfactory investigation until he finally decided to leave the novelty to rest. The bouquet rose from the wine bottle like a genie and filled the room with sparkling sunshine and the aromatic, medieval soil of Bordeaux. It pleased me to think that Montaigne might have drunk wine from the same vineyard, from the same offspring of grapes.

I went up to her bedroom and opened the closets. So many clothes, dresses, shoes, scarves, belts, hats. The drawers were stuffed with garter belts and black bikini panties that I had never been privy to seeing her wear. Soon the closet would be empty and I would leave it that way. Or leave it that way until I decided what to do with the house, too small for two, too large for one and a cat. She had left the bed unmade, the blankets and sheets twisted and tangled, as if they had been wrestling until they had given up, exhausted. I sniffed her pillow, which was heavy with perfume and dreams. Pascal came in and danced on the bed, where he had never been allowed.

I left him there stretched out on her pillow and went down to my study.

It welcomed me as never before. My desk with its teetering piles of books and loose sheets of notes and a printer and computer and a Chinese lamp, little pots full of outdated stamps and rubber bands, an instant-coffee jar crammed with red pencils, green paper clips heaped in a chipped blue teacup, a stapler, an old rotary phone, framed prints of Goya's *Puppet* and Poussin's *Echo and Narcissus*, Cézanne's *Bathers*, and van Gogh's *Wheat Field in Rain* greeted and accepted me without any conditions. I could sit at my desk all day and night and never again be presented with the obligation to clear or clean an inch of the disorder. Now, if I wished, I could even sweep away every single thing on the desk and leave it bare and hungry. Or I could chop up and burn the desk in the fireplace. I would wait for a cold night. There was plenty of time now to make decisions.

I went back to the living room and turned on the TV and madly switched channels, finding I liked everything that flashed across the screen, especially the Military Channel, where I watched a history of tank battles and decided I would rather have been in the navy if it had come to that. Montaigne, surprisingly, detested the sea, from where much contemplation springs. All the same, perhaps the swell of a wave and a splash of the brine might have made him a more dreamy man of the sky than the solid man of the earth, where he was so perfectly at home.

Later, watching another channel, I bought four Roman coins purporting to be authentic reproductions of the emperor Hadrian's young lover, Antinous, whose death he grieved until his last imperial breath. On another channel, I ordered a device that sucked wax from the ears. It was guaranteed that my hearing would improve within days. But then, after it was too late to change my mind, I realized I did not need or want to improve my hearing. Except for the music I love, I thought, I don't care to hear well at all. Most of what is said is better left unsaid and left unheard. It is the voices from the silent world of the self that matter, like the ones that Montaigne heard and wrote down in his tower room. I thought I might demolish the house now and build that tower in its place and live in the comfort of its invisible voices, and sit there and transcribe the voices as they came.

I grew bored with TV and realized that I missed reading my book of Montaigne's travels, that I missed him. Montaigne was someone I was sure that I could travel with, because he was someone whom I could leave or accompany whenever I chose. And there would be no recriminations, no arguments, no pulling this way and that about where to eat and how much to cool down or heat up the hotel room—or any room anywhere. I went back to my chair and opened Montaigne's book, sure that Pascal would soon arrive and jump up. But a half hour passed and he still had not come. I missed him and the game we played. So, after several more minutes, I went to find him. He was nowhere to be found. But the window to my wife's bedroom was open and I surmised he had left through it and to a world of his own making.

I was about to settle back to my reading when there was a strong knock at the door. I opened it to a man in a blue suit.

"Is she here?"

"Not presently," I said.

"Will she return presently?"

"Who knows?" I said.

"Well, I looked for her everywhere and thought she might have returned here," he said, peering in the doorway.

"Not here," I said, slowly closing the door.

"Do you mind if I come in a minute? Just to rest my feet."

"Have you been searching for her on foot?"

"Not at all," he said, nodding over to the cab standing before the house. "But I'm exhausted from looking for her."

"Come in," I said, not too graciously.

He went immediately to my favorite chair but before he could plunk himself down, I said, "That one's broken."

He sat down on the couch and gave me a sheepish grin. "Thanks, buddy."

I pretended to be reading my book but I was sizing him up, slyly, I thought. I did not find him remarkable in any way.

"Is she a reliable woman?" he asked.

"Absolutely. And punctual, too."

He looked about the room and folded his hands the way boys are told to do in a classroom. "Does she read all these books?"

"Some, but not all at once."

"That's very funny," he said with a little sarcastic smile. Then, changing to a more agreeable one, he asked, "Got something to drink? Worked up a thirst running around town looking for her."

"I just opened a bottle of wine you may like."

"Is it from California?"

"No."

"From France?"

"No, from New Zealand."

"I'll pass, then. How about a glass of water, no ice." I didn't answer. He stared at me a long time, but I waited him out. I noticed he wore burgundy moccasins with tassels and was without socks. That he had an orange suntan that glowed.

"She has me drop her off at the mall and says to come back and get her in an hour or two. But she never shows up."

"Was your meter running?"

"My Jag's in the shop. The cab's from my fleet."

"By the way, have you seen a cat out there in the street?"

"A salt-and-pepper one with a drooping ear?"

"Yes."

"No, I haven't." Then, in a shot, he added, "Is she your wife?"

"We're married," I said.

"She told me you were roommates."

"We do share rooms, though not all of them."

He stood up, pulled down his jacket, which seemed on the tight side, and came up close to me. "You're better off without her, pal. With all due respect, she's a flake, but the kind that suits me."

He went to the door and I followed, my book in hand, like a pistol. "Would you still like that water?" I asked in a most agreeable way.

"Don't tell her you saw me," he said.

"Cross my heart and hope to die," I said.

He gave me a long look, half friendly, half bewildered, half menacing. "You're not so bad for a dope."

He sped off in his cab—Apex. Twenty-four Hours a Day. We Go Everywhere. The street was empty. The sidewalk was empty. The houses and their lawns across the road were empty. The sky was empty. The clouds, too. I shut the door and returned to my favorite chair and went back to my book.

Montaigne wrote brief notes to his wife, describing his adventures with bedbugs and the summer heat, never referring to his urinary condition or to his pains, which worsened with each day. He noted that the Italians painted their bedpans with scenes from classical mythology, favoring those of Leda and her admiring swan. They were comforting, those bedpans, so unlike the severe white porcelain ones in France, which never thought to combine art with excrement.

I was near the end of the book and that left me in a vacuum for the remainder of the day. I thought that now that I was at large, I would need to plan for the evening and the night ahead. I would leave tomorrow to itself for now. But then the door swung wide open and she appeared, fancy shopping bags in hand.

"Well, aren't you going to help me?" I relieved her of two of the larger bags and settled them on the sofa. "There's another one on the porch," she said, as if I had been malingering. I retrieved it and another one at the doorstep, a large, round pink box.

She sat on the sofa and kicked off her shoes. She looked about, as if in an unfamiliar place. "What have you done?"

"To what?" I asked.

"To the room! It looks different. Did you change anything?"

"Nothing."

She looked at me suspiciously, then said, "Something's different."

"It knows you've left. Rooms always know when someone has left."

She pretended to yawn. "Sure."

"And they shift themselves to the new situation," I

added. "Like when a person dies in a bedroom and the walls go gray and cold. Or when a child is born and the room goes rosy and roomier."

"Has anyone been here since I left? I can smell that someone has."

"Now that you mention it, yes."

"Was he wearing a blue suit?"

"I didn't notice."

"Let me show you something," she said, removing her dress. She fussed about the shopping bags and pulled out a red skirt and red jacket with large buttons. "Whataya think?" she asked, fastening her last fat button.

"You look like a ripe tomato."

"It matches my handbag," she said, waving it before me. "I realized after I left this morning that my bag needs something to go with it."

"Everything matches and matches your hair, too."

"You've always had a good eye," she said.

"For you," I said in a kind of flirty way that I wasn't sure I meant.

"If you don't mind, I'm going upstairs to pack some things."

"Let me know if you see Pascal up there, please."

"That's another thing. I cringed every time you explained to a guest that Pascal was named after some French philosopher," she said, turning from me.

"If you had ever seen Pascal stare up at the night sky and give a little shiver, you'd understand," I said.

She was already halfway up the stairs and I wasn't sure she had heard me. But then she shouted down, "Did he say when he'll come back?"

I pretended not to have heard her. She came down the stairs again and said, "Well?"

"He didn't say. But his Jag is in the shop."

"I don't care about the books. You can keep them all," she said. "They prefer you anyway, like the cat."

"I named him Pascal, after his namesake, who asked for the patience to sit. I named him Pascal because he sits quietly in the window box and I can see in his eyes that he is training himself against his nature to learn to sit."

She gathered up the red dress suit and the handbag and, without a word, went back up the stairs. I returned to my book but my heart was not in it. Montaigne was on his way back to Bordeaux to his wife and his old life of solitude and voices. To his old known comforts. For all its vaunted claims, travel is a deterioration, taking minutes off one's life with every passing mile. So, for all his bravery, his condition worsened with each jolt of the carriage, with each bug bite and bad meal. By the time he finally arrived home, the blood in his urine had grown darker, the pain stronger, the loneliness greater.

I returned to the kitchen and to the remains of my lunch, still scattered on the table like the flotsam of a minor wreck. I sipped a glass of wine. It tasted of damp nails forgotten in a dank cellar. I sat there as the dusk filtered through the kitchen window, softening the edges of the table and the chairs and the hulk of the fridge. My hand looked like a mitten. Montaigne should never have left his tower, I thought, and gave voice to it in the shadows: "You should have stayed home," I said, advice given too late to an old friend.

Then I went to the door, thinking that Pascal might be there sitting on the step, waiting for me to let him in after his adventures in the wide world. Or maybe he would be just sitting and waiting for the night and the chill of its distant stars.

In the Borghese Gardens

For a while, near the end, living in Italy, Hawthorne grew less fascinated with persons and more with paintings. Paintings were new to him, had come to him late in his sober life—he had seen so few back home there in museumless Concord, with its dry, unadorned churches—but in the galleries and churches of Rome he feasted on whole brothels of color-drenched images. He peopled his last novel, *The Marble Faun*, with them, his descriptions of paintings in Roman galleries and churches weighing down the narrative and obliterating his flimsy cast of characters. Hawthorne had had his fill with characters—with people—by that time. He knew too much about them to want anymore to describe or to investigate their mystery. He was tired of telling the same old story of the dark human heart threatening always to shake order and reason, the minister's stiff dick in the forest, the reformer's vanity bulging under his rectitude.

While living in Italy, Hawthorne must have thought how far away America was from everything that softened life: the fall of golden light on a Roman pillar napping in the five o'clock dust, the dinner at the neighborhood café, lemon sherbet after, followed by an espresso burning like pitch. Life about him was burnished, even in winter, but the human heart was murderous and sex-driven even in Rome. But murder and sex burnished and giving off human heat. That is what *The Marble Faun* is all about, if only diagrammatically.

In Rome, Hawthorne trembled before "nude Venuses, Leda Graces . . . in short, a general apotheosis of nudity," as he put it. That is, I imagine he trembled, seeing before him what he had only dared in his imagination. Virginal Hester Prynnes stripped down to the waist, long hair trailing just above pink nipples. Zenobias on bare knees, arms knotted behind, head up, mouth parted. His friend Melville had seen all that and more, his conventional life in America barely masking his memories of youthful visits to faraway islands where beautiful women spread for him under the breadfruit tree.

How cold everything was back home, there in Concord. Himself, a cold stone in a pond. In Rome, even the hungry cats, sulking in the shadows of the Colosseum, were more joyful than the grave clan of Transcendentalists and other propertied visionaries peddling optimism and self-reliance. I think, in Italy, he gave up poking into the cold, dark corners of the human house and went out to the busy, noisy streets and gave himself to search for warmth and qualified joy, retreating from everything but paintings, which glowed with stories and needed no conversation. Unlike his family, who, after all, needed him and his voice, and unlike his few friends, who would have welcomed from him a kind word or two when, in fact, he no longer had words to give.

I do not forgive him for his coolness in the face of Melville's passionate storms, his hungry embrace of life. Melville came to visit Hawthorne in Rome and told him how he was driven to a kind of spiritual annihilation, how he could not believe or disbelieve in God. Without God, what is there but the endless sea and the clinging to life on a floating spar? How lonely he was, Herman, and how burning for some fatherly warmth and how self-deluded he was, seeking solace from a tepid cod. He who had once hunted whales—and had perceived their divinity—and had longed for love's cosmic merge had now winnowed down his pursuit of love to a New England fish swimming in Rome.

You would think Hawthorne would have missed Melville, his friendship, his devotion. But in Italy, he didn't really miss anyone or anything. His old desk in his attic, maybe, where he labored over his early stories, the shavings of his sentences scattered on the bare floor. Or the attic itself, where the winter light cast its moony silver shades even in the broiling summer. Nothing warmed him for too long, not even Rome in burning August. He was a coldish soul in any clime.

We made love in a little flat on the via della Croce,

and soon afterward we walked up to the Borghese Gardens and spread ourselves out under a giant tree. We were at the frayed end of our tether, in the lingering slow death of love. She could just as well have been making love to Hawthorne's feverless ghost in that little flat earlier that afternoon, a few tumbles to soothe the old writer and send him peacefully back to his grave. I had taken *The Marble Faun* with me to the park and, lying there on my back, I placed the book like a headstone on my chest.

I wanted to tell her I was sad that we were dying, that I could not imagine a coherent life without her, but we had gone through that drama enough all afternoon, until, as if on signal, we stopped speaking and went to bed, where various kinds of lovely deaths followed.

Now we were in the grass and spread out under a tree, our hands sometimes touching in postmortem affection, and I would imagine for a moment that we were right again, as we were once when we first came to Rome and thought the Tiber under our apartment was the river running through our Eden.

I wanted to turn and tell her my thoughts about Hawthorne and Melville and Rome, as I had the other ideas I had pronounced often over coffee and during long walks. Always the windy junior professor. But finally, I turned to her and said, "So of the two, which would you rather sleep with, Melville or Hawthorne?"

"Hawthorne, of course," she said. "Melville didn't like women anyway."

"Maybe just American women," I said, wanting to be unfair. She let it pass. That was one of her strengths, letting unpleasantries pass or pretending to, so that any blows I sent her just rebounded to me.

"I didn't really mean you personally," I added. But, of course, I had, wishing to wound her for wanting to leave me. When you're left, no matter how old you are, finally, you are always sixteen.

"Why don't you go back to reading your book," she said. "You've never been good at irony. You should know it doesn't work with me anyway."

"What does?" I asked, attempting to move closer again.

"Your friendliness," she said, "like when you were still courting me." She took my hand, but I felt no current passing through.

"It's a strange novel, this *Marble Faun*," I said, adjusting to my old role. "The characters are just fantastic shells for his old ideas and themes. And his long descriptions of paintings read as if culled from a guidebook. Everything about the novel is tired."

"He was about your age when he wrote it," she said. "He was still too young to be so tired."

"Rome makes you tired of wanting to do anything but live," I said.

"That's a cliché," she said. "Just because you feel at the end of your tether."

She rose and stood over me, casting a long shadow. She was returning to the apartment, she said, to pack and did not want me present while she did, because it would only make her sadder, when there was sadness enough to fill the day.

I'd stay in the park and read awhile, I said, and go back in a few hours, when she was finished packing, and take her to the airport. Accompanying her to the airport suggested something impermanent, a little trip from which she would shortly return and soon return to me. She wasn't sure it was a good plan, she said. It seemed only to prolong things, to stretch out the sadness.

What was she wearing then, standing over me in June? A thin red sweater, I think. And long, flowing skirt. Of course, she was right. Just prolong the sadness and stretch things out. But I protested, saying that whether I would or would not find her home when I returned, I hoped, in any case, she would be there. Maybe there and, who knows by what quirk and miracle, by what wondrous transformation, having changed her heart about leaving.

I tried to read as she walked away, but instead I watched her glide down the path leading ineluctably to the Spanish Steps and to all the rest of her life that would follow. It seemed only minutes later, before a chill rushed through the park and I looked about to find myself alone. I took the same path she had earlier and went down the empty Spanish Steps, empty steps and empty street below. I walked past the window where Keats once looked out, from the little apartment where he died, blood from his lungs flowing like a rushing stream in its sheeted bed.

Soon I wasn't walking anymore, but gliding along the vacant streets. Gliding as if on silent rollers—no bumps or halts, just smooth sailing as the day fell into dusk and the dusk into the burnt sienna powder of Rome. I looked about me, recognizing nothing familiar. I, who could have crossed Rome blind, was disoriented for the first time. But I was not alarmed, which was unusual for me, who is alarmed by the unusual and most all variations of the unexpected.

I halted at a window of a schoolhouse, where I saw myself at the blackboard doing additions. Four plus four equals eleven, I wrote. Seven plus seven equals ten, I wrote. The class was laughing at my mistakes. I felt the same shame I had then, all those years ago, and I wanted to call out the correct sums to myself, but the window would not open and I had already sat down, to the derision of my classmates, before I could shout out the right answer. My teacher, looking as she did thirty-five years ago, with the same ruby carbuncle on her forehead, came to the window and, without a word, yanked down the shade with a snap. I felt the chill of all those years at that school come over me again and I was glad to leave the window and the shamed self I had seen there.

The streets became avenues wider than bays and now I felt lonely and alone, a boy without a home port. But suddenly I was on a hill, where a white clapboard house rose on a cliff overlooking the city. The two women talking to each other on the porch turned to me in surprise.

"What are you doing here?" asked the one with white hair rolled into an old-fashioned bun, herself looking like the aunts who baked quince pies for church charities in old New England towns, Concord maybe, where the elms spread Puritan shade over the summer streets and the horse-drawn carriages trafficking them.

"Just thought I'd stop by," I answered in a familiar way, though I had not ever before seen her or the younger, beautiful woman beside her.

"On the way to where?" the young woman asked.

"It's not polite," the older woman said, "to ask questions so directly of strangers." She had a soft Sicilian accent, it seemed to me, though I had never been to Sicily.

"I was only asking!" she said in that voice teenagers use to show their exasperation with the minds of adults.

"I don't mind being asked," I said. "I was on my way home and found myself taken off course, as if the wind took my rudder and filled my sails."

That was a strange thing for me to say, never—to my

memory—having sailed, finding myself queasy even on a ferry ride from Manhattan to Staten Island, on the very few times I took that voyage.

"Well, we won't be keeping you, then, young man," she said, rather kindly, I thought. I was happy to be considered a young man. A man with time to start anew all the enterprises and dreams of my youth. To fall in love again with all the passion of youth; to be passionate again to meet new persons, seeing them as books burning to be read, all persons the authors of fabulous and unexplored selves.

"I'll keep you if she won't," the young woman said with a laugh the shape of a rose.

"How I'd love to stay! How I'd love to sit beside you at the fireplace—for I'm sure you have one—in the warmth of our home; how I'd love to stay until we all grow old and brittle like kindling wood waiting in the grate. But suddenly I remember I have an urgent appointment."

It was odd of me to have forgotten my appointment, but I blamed it on my being so caught up in the strangeness of my gliding peregrinations. But again, I wondered whether I ever had a rendezvous or had just imagined it at that moment on the porch, because in truth, I had no idea where or with whom this meeting was to take place.

I took my leave, turning about from time to time to give a wave of good-bye, until I finally reached a picket gate whiter than newly picked bones, and stopped to turn for one last farewell.

They were no longer there, the two, having gone into the house, I supposed. On the porch railing, where they had just been standing, now stood two crows, one large and the other medium, weaving and bobbing their heads and sending out the most doleful crowish cries. Recalling my cries when my son died far from home in a rooming house fire, his charred young bones fused with the iron bed.

Yes, I did have an appointment, but I did not remember—if I ever knew—where or with whom, but I have already said that. Not with her, who had left, who seemed, along with some old three-cent postage stamps and a tight ball of twine I had meant for my golden kite, already long away, gone far into the pocket of the century when I was a boy. A red sweater and green eyes under a shady tree.

He was sitting on a stone bench, waiting for me, in his long gray coat with double row of buttons, his granite hair matching his mustache, a stiff battlement above his thin lip. He was where I had last left him, or so it seemed. Perhaps he had left his post and had returned, but nothing in his demeanor said so. He could sit for hours in the same spot, expressionless, implacable—he was famous for it, even among the living.

"I hope I haven't kept you," I said. "It wasn't my intention to keep you, in any case."

He gave a shrug. I had no idea what it meant, but I felt its glacial breeze graze my face.

Finally, he asked, "Are you thinking of going back?"

"I wasn't thinking so," I said. "But I'm not sure. Why?"

"It's not like you to be late," he said, a bit ruffled, I thought.

"Are you?" I asked, disregarding his observation and worried he might return home and leave me with strangers, even those I had known for years.

"Well, some of the others have left recently," he said.

"Thoughts of home, thoughts of home, they come in many guises," I said, thinking of the afternoon's peculiar events and visits.

"Some veiled," he said with what I thought a smile.

Veils and concealments, his specialty, everything hidden and contained, like him, like his enviable work, earned through loneliness in dry rooms, by his not mistaking the sunshine in the window for human light, by his studying his pocket mirror and seeing the faces of the world reflected there.

(I have noticed, reading over the lines above, how odd a story this is. How it overtook me and led me about on its own will. Until it abandoned me suddenly and left me wondering why I was writing it at all and why I could no longer continue or finish it properly—with conviction. Left in the lurch, so to speak, with an interrupted conversation between two dead men on a stone bench. What was it they would go on to say to each other? I wonder.

For my part, I realize that the motor for this story was my preoccupation with *The Marble Faun*, with its bloodless characters and their isolation from a living world, recognizing in it my own increasing remove from people and my wish to live in and though paintings. Recognizing my increasing distance from my own country, with the exception of my city and the street where I live, my window facing Tompkins Square Park with its leafy elms. Recognizing also my remove from most everything but the books I have loved and the characters I knew there: the Consul, whose incapacity for orderly life and whose drunkenness I once thought noble; Prince Myshkin, with his Christ-like abnegations, his kindness to even the flies feasting on horse dung in the gutters; Ferdinand, whose lyrical journey I once, in my youth, took for my own as I stood on the Pelham Parkway train platform in the Bronx, where I saw the stars, like broken pieces of chalk, one by one, tumble through the night.

Recognizing in this incomplete story the elements of my exhaustion and my longing for childhood, however incapable I was then—as now—of adding up.

Recognizing here my wish for a porch of women, one mother, one lover, and my Melville-like yearning for a father who would explain to me the mysteries of the world.)

"I've been rereading your *Marble Faun* again," I said firmly to the man on the bench, as if to banish all other thoughts and discussion from the evening.

For the first time, he turned to me fully and nodded. For me to continue, I thought.

The Café, the Sea, Deauville, 1966

—1—

Natasha waved to him from her high window. He blew her a kiss. He checked his watch. He was already fifteen minutes late, but he decided to have a brandy at the café and burn away the rabbit-stew lunch still churning in his stomach.

—2—

Seagulls whirled in long loops, their reflections smashing into her window. She waved again before disappearing behind a flimsy red curtain.

"You know," he once had said after they had made love on their third rendezvous in her cold, vast apartment, "your curtains look like the ones in brothel windows in Amsterdam."

"You speak from firsthand knowledge, I suppose," she said.

"That's beside the point. Why dress your window like a whore's?" He regretted saying that, apologized, and later bought her a large blue tin of her favorite caviar.

"I hope it cost you plenty," she said.

"Not enough for my stupidity," he answered, hoping he sounded sufficiently contrite. "You are far from a whore or vulgar," he added.

"Not as far as my curtains go, it seems."

"No need for irony. I know that you soar above me. You are the apotheosis of high culture. You are the total artwork, the *Gesamtkunstwerk* that Wagner dreamed of creating."

He was unsure about his German pronunciation, but she did not correct him, and he had hoped, in any case, that she would be impressed with his smattering of opera culture, and he considered adding, "Let me take you to see *Tristan und Isolde* the next time it comes to Paris." But he reckoned the expense would be above his means—the first-class train round-trip, the best orchestra seats, the high-class dinner after, and then a fine room at a fine hotel. She was rich enough to travel without advance planning or thought of expense. But she seldom left her apartment or her street. So what good was her money? He would have loved to travel—to live—without a care. Not to have to settle for a middle-grade hotel with faded carpeting and suspect sheets, to be able to take an aeroplane anywhere, just on a whim, on a desire—what more was there to life but an elegant life?

"Thank you, for the compliment," she said. "It struck a note."

"You have your own power and beauty to pick and

choose. I don't know why you even give me a tumble," he said.

She laughed. "If you think that, you know very little of life and nothing of women."

He checked his watch again—noticing a crack in its crystal—before entering the empty café, where Alfred stood waiting for no one.

–3–

The Longines Conquest, with a green lizard strap, burned his wrist. His wife had given him the watch some birthdays ago—"for the man I love," she had said—and it told him the wrong time to punish him for his infidelities and it made him think of death three times a day and at night after dinner and again before slipping under the bedcovers.

He could always blame the tricky watch for his being late, but Natasha would know he was lying.

–4–

"Good afternoon, Monsieur Alfred," he said to the barman, who was standing by the window and looking out to the sea.

"The usual?" Alfred asked without turning and still at the window, writing in a small green notebook.

He had always found Alfred polite enough, cordial enough, but never embracing of his clients, or at least the few he had ever encountered there at the bar or seated at the old-fashioned, upholstered red leather banquettes with marble-top tables and black wrought-iron legs. He never understood what she saw in the café, why she had once said, "That's the only place I want to be other than my bedroom or my kitchen. It's my sea cave, and if Alfred changes it, I will die."

"It's very gloomy," he once ventured to comment. "Narrow like a coffin for a tall, narrow person," he had added for emphasis.

"I wonder," she said, "if I can make it my mausoleum?"

"It's already Alfred's," he said, thinking that she must never, never die. That he would never allow it.

"Not today, Alfred. A brandy will do, I think. Yes, something solid, fortifying but not medicinal. Something celebratory, even."

The brandy was surprisingly rough, and he thought of making a small fuss, but finally he decided to say, "Alfred, what is your best brandy, and will you have one with me?"

"Gladly, but in spirit," Alfred said.

–5–

He swirled the brandy in the snifter, sniffed, sipped, smiled. He made a pleased face and an approving nod. But it was all show, because all he was thinking about was his watch.

–6–

He sported a yellow maple-wood cane fashioned in Vermont, where he dreamed one day of visiting and seeing for himself the sweet sap ooze down from the maple trees. America, where trees bled sugar and people lived in yellow maple-wood cabins and sang hymns before dinner. He had read that. The simple life. He longed for it.

A simple life with her in her blue stone-floor kitchen and its collection of aging copper pots she never used but left hanging on hooks from the ceiling, as they were when her mother died. And the samovar, too, like a fat-bellied silver god of the kitchen.

It made him uncomfortable that once, in their rush to couple, the samovar had watched them making love on the kitchen floor and he had imagined that the pots would fall down on them for punishment.

"There is a kind of sanctity to the kitchen that we should perhaps respect," he once said to her. "Everything has its place, the bedroom for love, the toilet for you know what, and the kitchen for cooking, no?"

"I never cook in the kitchen or anywhere else," she replied. "Unless you consider boiling water cooking."

He kept on his hat, a weathered Borsalino that had belonged to his father, a country doctor who made house calls even in the deepest winter and never remarried. He thought of his father every time he put on and took off the hat.

One day he would go to Milan and buy a new Borsalino and store the old one in his closet for good luck. And maybe he'd also buy a new suit; his workaday gray flannel with pinstripes sagged at the shoulders and looked tired, although his polished new shoes mirrored the sky and made him seem current. His father's shoes had always been bruised and caked with mud and blades of grass from his country rounds. What good was it to be an educated doctor and look like a rustic, a farmer, a bumpkin married to the earth?

She had chosen his beautiful shoes for him on their tryst in London, in a shop on Jermyn Street, where rows of burnished leather shoes sat in the window like saints. "Those," she had said, "get those, and get a black umbrella and keep it rolled tightly as the Englishmen do."

–7–

He was still lingering over his second brandy when she emerged from her building. His watch explained he was now more than thirty-five minutes late. She came close up to the window and looked in; he smiled and saluted her with his brandy. Instead of walking into the café, to him, as he had expected, she sped away toward the promenade.

–8–

She took a seat at a table on the empty, chilly café terrace. She enjoyed the cold, the gray dampness of Deauville, where the old stone houses kept their winter iciness even in summer. She imagined that she would light the fireplace when she returned home and not answer the phone.

She ordered a double espresso, *bien serré*, she said, because she liked the sound of the words, and opened a newspaper someone had left on the chair beside her. It was three days old, but she was glad that everything she read had already happened, as in a film or an absorbing novel by Simenon, which she regretted not having brought along with her to the café.

—9—

His father would return from his house calls late at night and sit in the kitchen smoking his pipe, an encrusted briar from Algeria. Sometimes he would fall asleep at the table, his stethoscope still draped about his neck, his dinner half eaten.

"The trick," his father had once said, "is never to stop moving, so that life passes quickly and slowly at the same time."

—10—

Without asking her permission, a young man sat down in the chair facing her. "May I engage you in conversation?" he asked.

She raised her newspaper higher. Then he asked the same in Italian, and again in English.

—11—

"Here's what I think, Alfred," he said, "brandy flattens the appetite for love. But calvados quickens its hunger."

"After fifty, one should only drink warm milk with half a spoon of honey," the barman said.

"I still have some time, then, Alfred."

"Of course. I myself have only started drinking milk recently, a decade ago."

"Do you drink alone, Alfred? Or do you have a wife?"

"A wife? No."

"Do you want one?"

"No."

"What are you attached to, then?"

"The café. And the window, of course."

"Let me have a calvados, then. I'll toss you for it."

The barman laughed. "A spinning coin makes me dizzy."

He looked out the window, wondering if he should leave and go after her or wait for her to come to him, whereupon he would apologize and offer her a kir royale, her favorite drink.

"Do you like your profession, Alfred?"

"It is the only one I have known or have ever wished for. And you?"

"I thought I'd be a doctor, like my father. But I came to realize there is no point in a doctor trying to keep people alive, because in time we all will die anyway."

"Yes, but some people like to linger as long as possible. Anyway, there's no telling when it will come. I've witnessed two of my steady clients die before they finished their first drink. But mostly, we are all leaves waiting for our season to fall from the tree."

"That's very philosophical, Alfred, the leaves, the trees, the cycle of life and death. But it's not very comforting, and forgive me, but I think I have heard all that before."

"Yes, it's an old song. As for comforts, I think there are very few. In any case, may I offer you another calvados?"

—12—

She lowered the newspaper. The young man was handsome, his suntan richly even, his nose slightly bent, offsetting what would have made his good looks quickly boring. His blue blazer fit too tightly, and so did his white shirt, open at the throat. He sleeked his hair back like a tango dancer in an Argentinian movie of the thirties.

—13—

"Would you like another espresso?" the young man asked.

"No, thank you."

"A glass of wine?"

She folded the paper and gave him a long look, from which he did not flinch or look away. "A Pouilly-Fuissé or a Sancerre," she said, adding, "No, a kir royale."

"That's an elegant choice. Of course, it would be from you."

—14—

A propeller aeroplane circled overhead as if uncertain of its destination. She wished it would drop into the sea and drown along with its annoying buzz. She hated aeroplanes and hated travel. London, maybe, from time to time, because its wet grayness was like staying home. But perhaps one day she would take a train to Russia and see what all the mystery was about, all that vast gray, vast space, and drunken melancholy that she had read about in those old novels with their murky, noble souls talking without reserve to the heart of life. "When you read a Russian novel, especially Dostoevsky's *The Idiot*, you learn all you need to know about life," her mother had told her, drinking tea with a sugar cube between her teeth. She herself had read the same Russian novels, keeping it a secret from her mother, for fear she would say, "How dare you trespass into my private world?"

The damp sea breeze chilled her. She shivered and liked it.

"Take my jacket," he said, without removing it.

—15—

"Have you," she asked the young man, "ever read Miguel de Unamuno's *Tragic Sense of Life*?"

"No need to. I know life's tragic."

"Have you ever read a book?"

"No and I never will."

"Can you read?"

"Certainly. But I have no wish to."

He tapped his foot until her sharp look ordered him to stop.

–16–

She wore black stockings with seams. A green skirt, a classic Chanel that her mother had left for her in its original box. The skirt smelled faintly of mothballs. Her sleeveless straw yellow sweater, a cashmere woven in Scotland that she had bought in London at Westaway & Westaway, loved her.

The straps of her high-heeled black shoes bound her ankles like sadistic vines. "Wear those shoes whenever we make love," he had said. She had forgotten to change them in her rush to leave the house.

–17–

Earlier that afternoon, he had been taken to lunch by his colleagues at the law office to celebrate his fiftieth birthday. He ordered a frisée salad to start, followed by a rabbit stew with turnips and a crème caramel for dessert. The espresso was bitter. The calvados made up for it.

A young colleague asked him, "What is the secret to a good life?" He was flattered to be asked but shrugged his shoulders as if to say, How would I know? He had thought of saying, "Keep moving so life passes quickly and slowly at the same time," but he was afraid of sounding sagelike and open to mockery. He was woozy when he left the restaurant and aglow with good feelings. He announced that he was the luckiest man alive to have such colleagues. But he saw that he was running late to his rendezvous and was glad to leave them chattering happily on the sidewalk and to find a taxi so quickly. A thought came to him as he stepped in the cab and, for a moment, he considered turning to the young man who had asked his advice and saying, "Do not expect anything. Not even unhappiness."

–18–

She enjoyed his thick weight on her, the apple aroma of calvados in his pores. She liked that he kept his watch on in bed while all else of him was naked white. She liked that he was neither young nor old but at the moment of fullness before he turned unattractively ripe.

She liked how sometimes he would turn from tender to cruel, his voice commanding her to undress, to bend, to stand by the wall with her legs spread apart. "Do what you want to me, so long as you do it only with me," she had said not long after they had met.

–19–

"Married?" she asked, after deciding the young man was handsome.

"Yes."

"No ring?"

"No need to blazon one's life."

"May I ask your profession?"

"I'm a professor of the tango," the young man said, adding, "I would be honored to give you lessons."

"What makes you think I don't already know how to dance the tango?"

"I can tell from your legs."

—20—

"Let's go for a walk," the young man said, half rising from his seat.

"Not now. Maybe some other time."

"When?"

"When it's another time."

—21—

His watch also made him overeat. It made him sing like a mouse in the shower. It made him want to run from his life, all expenses paid, and fly to Brazil and sleep in a straw hut by a giant, frightening river and eat fish and fat corn roasted over a pit.

—22—

How much time had passed since he entered the café, he did not know. His watch had stopped entirely, rigor mortis setting in at 4:07. Now he had an excuse to get rid of it and all the trouble it caused him. He was about to leave to find her, when she passed by the window, glanced at him, laughing, young, immortal, on the arm of a slender, young, immortal man. At first, he thought he would go after her, but he quickly envisioned the vulgar scene that would ensue. It would be better to wait some while before trying to beg her forgiveness, to try first sending her flowers, white roses, nine, to make it up to her. And when he was with her again, bringing her another tin of caviar, the thought of which made him grind his teeth at the expense. Or maybe he would never try, after her going off with a boy.

"Good-bye, Alfred," he said.

"Don't forget your cane," Alfred replied, walking to the window.

–23–

He reached the sea and its flatness. Not a wave, not a ripple, not a crease. The sea was dozing, hoarding up its passion. There were no umbrellas, no chairs on the beach. The cabanas were boarded up; the houses shuttered and locked down, silent, bored, waiting for summer and the exciting return of their tenants. A three-legged black dog ran up and down, wheeled and wheeled, and, howling, crashed into the water. Seagulls. He tightened his coat. He searched for his gloves. But he found instead a book he had bought for her, *Dirty Snow*, because she read Simenon by the dozens while smoking in bed.

"I hate Russian novels," she had told him once, apropos of nothing, when he was about to enter her.

–24–

"Do you still make love to your wife?" she asked one day at the zoo.

"From time to time, as a courtesy," he said.

"To her?"

"To duty."

–25–

She watched the afternoon cling to her window, then fall away. The young man in her bed snored. It rained, smearing her windows, but she still could see the café below breaking into its first evening light.

It had rained like this one night when her mother had said, "When I'm gone, do what you wish with this place; it will be yours, of course. But please keep some of it the way I leave it. Above all, please keep the samovar where it is in the kitchen. As long as it is there, I am, too."

"Your ghost, Mother."

"My spirit," she had replied.

The phone did not ring. She supposed that he would not call so soon, in any case, but she wished he would so that she could berate him for keeping her waiting. Tell him never to call her again. Tell him he had done her a favor, because now she had found a man who knew what to do in bed and he could do it forever.

She was chilled and went to the kitchen to make tea. The Russian samovar stood atop a teak table draped with a heavy red damask cloth that fell to the edge of its portly nineteenth-century legs. She nodded to the samovar and lit the kettle on a stove with seven burners and on which her mother had stewed red meat and cabbage following a Russian recipe. Her mother had studied and spoke Russian but had never gone to Russia. Her mother read Russian novels and poetry in Russian and drank tea from a thick glass. She'd once said, "Only the Russians know life."

"What is it that they know?" she had asked, annoyed that her mother would believe that about a people who drank vodka without nuance and ate radishes without butter.

–26–

"How much did you enjoy that?" the young man asked on waking, his eyes shut.

At first, because she did not like his presumption, his preening maleness, she thought to reply, "Perhaps you are more proficient at giving tango lessons." Instead, she said, "If you want coffee or something to eat, you will have to go out."

"Coffee, sure. But let's drive to Rome, where the coffee has taste."

"Are you old enough to drive?"

"Yes, and with my own car." He had opened his eyes and was beaming like a proud boy, the teacher's pet.

"I don't like Italy. Or Spain, or England. I like it only here in this city, in this apartment. Or in the café across the street, but never after five."

She was starting to dress when the phone rang and

would not surrender. She lifted the receiver and let it drop. It rang again. She unplugged the phone and, for safe measure, left the receiver off the cradle. "I've decided," she said, sliding into bed beside him, "to change my routine, so there's time for coffee or a drink after."

"It's good to be flexible," he said, opening her robe.

"But I do not like to talk over coffee."

"Why talk anyway," he said, "now that it's been done."

—27—

He looked up at his apartment window and its mellow, homey glow. Then, after a few moments of lingering in the rain, he took the stairs slowly, counting the steps. He was glad that the elevator was out of order, because he feared it, not that it would fall but that, on a whim, it would decide to compress its walls and crush him like an iron maiden.

He hung his hat on the rack to dry, and, even before he took off his wet overcoat, his wife said, "I made you your favorite for dinner, rabbit and turnips in white wine. For your birthday, my sweet wet bear."

She was wearing her black going-out dress and a cultured-pearl necklace he had given her on their tenth anniversary. He kissed her and gave her an extra hug and kissed her again. For a moment, he thought to say, "That's too bad; I had rabbit for lunch." He decided instead to say, "How thoughtful of you, my dear," giving her a kiss on both cheeks.

He had drunk too much wine at lunch and too much calvados at the café and he felt heavy in his bones and had wet cement for blood.

His wife was speaking to him very pleasantly, but it did not matter. "You are still a young man," she said, thinking he was brooding at yet another birthday.

"Young enough still, I suppose," he said, feeling, as he said it, a breeze of time whiz by and take another year from him in its wake.

After dinner, in bed that night, he said, "Maybe we should go to the mountains this summer?"

"You hate the mountains. You always say you hate the mountains."

"Yes, but sometimes we must try new things before we dive into the winter of our life."

–28–

The rain pelting the window kept him awake. It made him imagine himself dead and the rain leaching into his casket until whatever decomposed bits were left of him floated like suds in the bath. Also, the two rabbits jumped in his stomach, the lunch rabbit and the dinner rabbit. Also, he wondered if she would ever want to see him again or if this time, by keeping her waiting, he had gone too far.

His wife raised herself on her elbows and stared at him.

"Indigestion?"

He spoke in a low voice that she was not accustomed to. "Never be in love or love too much."

"Are you in love with someone now?"

"No."

She stayed silent for a long time. Finally, she said, "The mountains would be agreeable."

–29–

Alfred was most happy when the café was empty and the sea was flat and biding its time to go wild. Above all, he liked to stand by the window as the afternoon light shrank into the edge of night—this light—and to write in a green notebook, where he gathered up all the pieces and fragments of the day that he could recall, even the smallest thing: the sunlight on a hand as it raised a glass or the cracked crystal of a watch and the shadow it made on the dial. Or the way a man regards a woman from behind the café window as she crosses the street, as if the glass shielded his hungry gaze from being seen. Or the way a man drinks hunched at the bar, his black hat crowning the yellow cane beside him like a silent drinking partner.

He looked up at her apartment window and was lucky. The light behind her as she stood at the rain-smeared window outlined her beauty. She was always beautiful.

She never made cozy small talk and self-indulgent chatter as did most of his regulars, as if he were their friend, their confidant.

She had overstepped only once when she was drunk, and had cried about her dead mother and rambled on about the beauty of the Russian soul. "Only the Russians understand melancholy, without which the soul starves. The falling snow, the crushing cold, the great distances, the birch trees in the moonlight—the Russian soul, who knows it better than I?" she had said.

There was more of the same until she tottered and almost fell off her stool; he half walked, half carried her to her building and to her apartment, where she collapsed in her bed. He had removed her shoes before leaving and left a light on in the hall lest she wake up frightened in the dark. He had rushed to leave: The vast apartment with its empty rooms and no furniture or carpets or standing lamps or pictures to befriend the naked walls had given him a chill that only his café and a glass of hot milk could warm. He had much to enter in his green notebook when standing by the café window; he took his bowl of breakfast coffee as the sea swelled to meet the first morning light.

She apologized the next day, bringing him a gift. A Simenon novel about a man who, one day, telling no one, taking nothing, simply walked out of his life, leaving his small, successful business, his three employees, and faithful wife to puzzle over where he had disappeared to. He had enjoyed the book but wondered if it was something she had at hand and gave to him without a thought, an impromptu token of apology. If not, why would she ever have imagined he would have liked to read about a man who turned away from his life, taking the first train that pulled into the station and, without a plan, alighting in a remote village unknown to him and whose only light, at ten at night, came from a café with three drunks and a whore?

He himself was too settled, too happy in his café with its window to the sea, ever to leave. All the life that mattered flowed through that window and all the people in the world were winnowed down to the few who came to the café.

Though he was fearful of the time when he would be too old or too ill to tend to the café and stand by its window, he had a plan that comforted him. One day, he would sit himself in his club chair in his cozy room above the café and, with a warm glass of milk on a silver tray by his side, pore over all the years of green notebooks, one by one, savoring the pages line by line as if he were a stranger who had discovered them in a trunk beached from a schooner drowned at sea.

Lives of the Artists

SHE WALKED IN FROM HER STUDIO, her sneakers streaked with wet grass, and plunked herself down at the kitchen table.

"Why the long face?" I asked.

"Do you ever think," she said, "about the lives of artists? Do you ever think how many of us there are, there were, all of us smearing color on a cloth or a panel of wood or on some surface or another? Like children."

"There are many."

"Or on a cave wall in dim light, while some beast is waiting outside in the cold for you to come out, only to gut you."

"It must be fun, or why do it?"

"Well, I'm here talking to you and it's not much fun at all, so why am I doing it?"

"Stumps me."

Outside the window, snowflakes spiraled about, as if deciding whether or not to crash fully down or to delay some weeks until it was officially winter. Victor was out there cavorting in the garden, a size 24 flat between his teeth.

"That's exactly the brush I needed," she said. "He's not letting go of it."

"Nothing else will do?"

"Of course not! When your heart's set on a brush, that's it for the day. You would feel the same way about your pipe."

"I don't smoke a pipe."

"Well, if you did."

"How would you be if we skip lunch today?" I said, anxious to get back to a clear day of writing.

"That's fine. I have a guy coming over for a studio visit anyway."

"A guy?"

"Paul, from that gallery. He's interested in my work and he said he may put me in a group show next fall."

"Of course, he's in love with you."

"Don't be a jerk."

"Or he wants to sleep with you."

"So, that's why he's interested in my work?"

"One cannot escape the erotic component of relationships."

"You're just jealous and hiding it behind a ridiculous theory."

"Probably. Hope he'll put you in the show. It's a good gallery."

"Do you want to drop in and say hello before he leaves?"

"If I'm not still working."

"Still that book about artists?"

"Could be," I said.

"Why are you so slippery?"

"Shall we go out to dinner tonight, dear?"

"To that phony French joint with the Piaf music?"

"*Pas de tout.* I was thinking of a new place, a Spanish-Uruguayan restaurant that just opened in Kent."

"A Spanish-Uruguayan restaurant in Connecticut? Are you joking?"

"Not at all. Its cuisine is an amalgam of classic French and European dishes with distinctly Uruguayan elements, creating, in the process, something unique and vibrant—and tasty."

"Did you just make that up?"

"From the *Times* review. Regional section. But I supplied the final word." I could see Paul coming out of his Audi A7 and crossing the garden to the studio. He was better dressed and spiffier than when I'd run into him a few years ago. Now, he was a player with his own small but influential gallery on West Twenty-sixth Street. He had an eye for the young, the new, and the soon to be forgotten. He was stepping gingerly in the grass to avoid getting his polished shoes wet in the brush of morning snow.

"You'd better get going," I said. "He's here."

She kissed me on the cheek. "Love you," she said. And then, pivoting at the door: "How do I look?"

"Ravishing."

"You old fool," she said.

I took the stairs and went directly up to my study. I could see them below through the studio's French windows and generous skylight, him sitting on the sagging cane chair, her standing, the two chatting. After some minutes, she started turning about, one by one for his judgment, the paintings that faced the wall like punished students. She smiled a confident smile, while her heart, I was sure, ticked between hope and trepidation.

I let down the blinds, lest the observer change the observed, and returned to my work—a little book of vignettes about artists I had loved since I was a young man, many years ago. After all my years of writing about art, I wanted once, before I died, to bring myself clearly into the text. All art writing is personal, finally, no matter how disinterestedly it is dressed up.

I hoped that when I had assembled all the vignettes, the underlying foundation of what I had loved and what was common to the artists I had loved would disclose itself to me and to others, namely and principally to my young wife. My little book was about artists whom she might see as cautionary or exemplary models for her life. It was my legacy for her.

I tried to put away all distracting thoughts, tried not to think of the unfolding drama below me in the studio, and began to review my previous day's work.

Rousseau's Clouds

In all his Paris life, Rousseau never traveled beyond a few feet of his Montparnasse neighborhood, or maybe he crossed the Seine to visit the Louvre and to daydream there. To save tram fare, he walked everywhere, sometimes with his paintings strapped to his back to hawk to dealers.

He made paintings of jungles he had never seen and portrayed lions in deserts he had never set foot upon. He had found on his visits to the Jardin des Plantes the wild jungle foliage that crowded his paintings; he transported the lions and leopards and monkeys from his safaris at the zoo at the garden to his canvases. That would have been his longest walk and his most tiring excursion. Perhaps that is why the animals in his paintings look so loopy and half asleep. The figures in his paintings? He had imagined most of them or had seen them on postcards of peasants in their Normandy costumes. His skies resembled crumpled backdrops in a provincial theater. Did he ever, on his way through the narrow Parisian streets and alleys, look up and see a puffy, living cloud floating on its way to somewhere?

Young artists were stupefied by his lack of technical skill, puzzled by his naïveté bordering on idiocy.

Contemporary movements were dedicated to dynamiting official art and its darlings, like Bouguereau and Puvis de Chavannes. Meanwhile, Rousseau's aspiration—his dream!—was to make the very art that the radical hotheads hated; in his mind, he was doing exactly that, but his paintings, with their improbable scenes and mis-en-scène and stiffly painted figures and clouds like bricks of white soap, said otherwise.

I opened the blinds and looked down and saw them now both standing; he nodded from time to time as a new canvas was turned about to face him. On the third painting, he opened his arms expansively, as if to say how much he liked it. She smiled, reservedly, I thought; I admired her composure. But then again, I admired everything about her.

Rousseau went his own fantastical way, and his pictures sold for little to zero. One was bought by Picasso for five francs, a portrait of a woman he had stumbled upon in the rear of a junk shop. With Guillaume Apollinaire, Picasso organized a banquet in homage to Rousseau and to show the painting he had bought and loved and that he kept within easy view all his life. Was it a joke? some wondered. This painting of a woman with a pinhead stuck on a huge black dress and against a sky that wanted sun? The singularity that Picasso had seen in Rousseau's painting eluded others. Some immediately apprehend such singularities, and it might take others years to discern them. I would tell her, "Let your paintings rest and ripen—then they will be ready for fresh eyes."

The banquet, an ebullient riot packed with artists and poets—even Gertrude Stein showed up—gained Rousseau a few straws of recognition, but he was too insular, perhaps too proud to ignite them into a flame. "I do not promote myself," he said to Picasso, the greatest self-promoter, "my work does that for me."

Better that Rousseau did not try to sell himself; in his bumbling, half-shy, half-vainglorious way, he would have failed. "The boundary between successful and unsuccessful self-promotion is very fine," I would tell her. "If done poorly, you are reviled for your efforts."

Rousseau lived in such a dingy place that even the sunlight approached his filthy window like a timid beggar at a wedding feast. Rodents hated the dump. "Mice," Picasso quipped, "take pity and offer him cheese." One day, in desperation, Rousseau invested his pathetic, meager savings into a scheme to defraud the Bank of France. He lost every dime. He barely escaped prison for what the police claimed to be his part in the fraud. As a young man, he had already been imprisoned for petty theft and he knew what he would have faced. Not that a cell would have been worse than his room, but would they have let him paint?

Finally, none of this mattered, the squalor, the almost recognition, the penury: His paintings meant more to him than the two wives who had died in protest of their husband's indifference to poverty and its blight on their conjugal life. Why did he ever marry? The prix fixe meals of a greasy stew and a demicarafe of a rough Sardinian wine at a café down the street were his Versailles and, as for glory, he was sure he was destined for the Pantheon—Picasso was behind him in the line.

When Rousseau died, a few admiring artists had to pay the costs of his funeral, with its flimsy coffin, and even had to cough up a tip for the two grave diggers. Seven people showed up at the burial. One, who had come drunk on calvados, had come in error.

Is a reduced life worth a few smears on a canvas? Is it worth the paint, even? I would ask. I would ask her.

Monet's Ponds

Once Monet made Giverny his home, he never left. He had designed a flower garden and an artificial pond bulging with lily pads for his models—he could paint all morning and easily walk a few feet to his home and have a good full lunch that could kill a giant or have a coffee anytime he wanted, brewed strong enough to make his heart pound. He had long ago learned that he need not change his subject matter to give his art variety and newness: By painting the same scene in different light, each work told a different story. Or was it that, as some said, in staying fixed in his niche, he had found his way to stay rich and live well?

His paintings sold off the rack to Japanese and

American collectors who fancied lilies floating in scum-free ponds and virginal flowers in lush gardens. Monet let them believe what they wished, but he confided to a friend, "Where they imagine flowers and lily pads, I see splotches of color floating in space." He received honors and got thick in a solid, prosperous way and then even thicker and even more prosperous. His work, like him, grew larger in size. As he grew older, he became ever more snug in his already snug nest, where notables came to pay him homage—even Clemenceau, the premiere of France.

He was the proof, a few said, that a genius need not be impoverished and tormented and that material ease was—or could be—the soil for creating beauty. Some of his fellow artists—hunkered down in airless, smoke-clogged cafés in Paris—said that Monet was no longer painting art but was painting money, and they cited his bourgeois life as evidence of the disease of success. The disease spread, one of his collectors noted, with seemingly no ill effect on the patient or on his art.

"Live at the margin," I would tell her. "Don't let yourself get too close to the comfortable center, but don't live too far from its warmth. If you have the choice, don't starve like Rousseau; don't stuff yourself like Monet."

Love Among the Palm Fronds

Gauguin turned his back on Paris and went far afield to Tahiti, where it took months to have canvases and paints and brushes shipped to him, but the bother was worth it. After all, he had achieved what most artists dream of, a place to live and paint rent-free for next to nothing in a hut of his own making. Unlike Rousseau, he did not have to walk to a park to see exotic flora; it was spread before him right outside his thatched hut's naked window. He did not waste time, as he would have in Paris, in grubby cafés in the company of fellow artists and what he called their grubby aesthetic quarrels and jealousies. He called his hut the Maison du Jouir, where his lovers came and went freely and for the pleasure of it, at least on his side.

He was alone but never had to worry about love—he was always in love under a generous sky. He was faulted for escaping everything that had tied him down to a bourgeois life, his wife and children included. He wasn't one to let the envious trouble him. There was never an artist as self-sufficient and as selfish as he, but, at the end, look what came of it.

For all that self-sufficiency, he was lonely all the same, lonely even for the rot of a Europe that had traded innocence for railroads. Lonely even for the vast warehouse of art that was Paris, and where slowly his reputation was gaining ground. He could have returned a legend. Instead, he stayed, sick, half-blind, painting in his hut to the end. With whom was he in dialogue, with what culture? What faith in himself did he have that all his loneliness would, at the end, pay off, that he would not be remembered, if at all remembered, as merely a sojourner in the exotic?

He had pinned a postcard of a painting by Puvis de Chavannes to his hut's door—even in a leafy world away, he could not escape his longing for Europe and the culture it represented. Perhaps in compensation, he invented a grand formula that transcended time and place. On a wooden board, he carved his last and summary message to the world: "Always be in love and always be happy."

"Isn't that what we all want, Paul?" I would have asked. "To be in love and to be happy, even for a little while?" Was she in love and happy with me, still? I wondered, too, at the outcome of the scene below, where her work was being decided. I resisted taking a peek out my window, but I knew my resolve would not last long.

Cézanne's Rock

He was impressed with fame and trembled before it: That the illustrious Monet had deigned to speak to him had left him dizzy with gratitude. Better for him, then, to retreat to the hinterlands of the burning, peasant south and not let his adulation for the famous and his own low visibility cloud his mind, injure his work. Cézanne left Paris, where he was thought to be a nobody, and went back home to Aix to get things done.

He had a small income his father had bequeathed him, so that he was *disponible*, an artist at large and with nothing to occupy him but his work. With nothing expected of him, he was free to change the world. Nothing but his work mattered, and no one mattered. Like Gauguin, he, too, had left a wife and a child behind to paint unencumbered and with rare interruption. When his mother, whom he loved, died, Cézanne did not take a break from painting even to attend her funeral. "If you leave your work once, you will leave it again under any pretext," he was supposed to have said. Nothing could have better described him than Manet's line: "You are not a painter if you don't love painting more than anything else."

He rose every morning at first light to go to early Mass, where he devoutly lit a two-cent candle and sent his prayers to heaven. He had winnowed down his life to the ecstasy of painting—another form of praying. He left the church and town behind and trudged up a path through wooded hills to obsess over Mont Sainte-Victoire, a distant mountain pile without majesty and unworthy of an artist's or poet's comment. But he never had to fret about the model rotting like a band of apples on a table, or getting fatigued, or yawning, or fidgeting about and ruining the pose as he, day by day, went about deconstructing a simple elevated rock into planes, into a revolution in art.

❖

She had asked me some weeks ago to come to her studio to see a painting she had just finished. I sat before it and took some moments to respond, wanting to give her and the painting the full measure of my thought.

"You obviously don't like it."

"Not true," I said.

"What is it, then?"

"It takes time to find your soil."

"My soil? The gallery, the museum, and the art school?"

"Your conversation with art," I might have replied, though it would have been unwise of me. That was for her to discover or not.

I might have told her how, one year before his death, Cézanne had petitioned the Louvre to be allowed to paint in the Poussin room. He believed that in his paintings, he saw that Poussin had left him a message: I can only go just so far, Paul. These structures of mine, I know they lead elsewhere. Take them where they must go. And Cézanne did, turning nature into forms with cousins in heaven, taking what he saw in Poussin's latent geometry and making it manifest, transforming the raw and amorphous into immutable forms.

They were now standing in the snowy garden. He put his hand on her right shoulder and kept it there for a little too long, I thought; he smiled a smile the size of an ocean, while she remained impassive, unreadable or perhaps all too readable.

He withdrew his hand from her shoulder and extended a handshake, which she slowly accepted but withdrew as soon as he placed his other hand on her other shoulder. I wanted to applaud.

He nodded, made a little bow, which she returned. They exchanged words, each smiling pleasantly, and he walked away to his car, mute. He waved before climbing in. I shut the blinds.

I heard her enter the house and ramble about below and thought it best to let her come up and tell me in her own time what had happened. I kept waiting, until I could no longer wait and went down.

She was sitting at the kitchen table, a glass of white wine—either celebratory or commiserative—in hand.

"Hello, chum," she said, raising her glass to me. "Has Victor come back?"

"Not even his bark."

"I depend on that bark, you know. He's my most honest critic. I've heard him growl at paintings he doesn't like and bark at the ones he does," she said. "But maybe I got it backward. Or maybe he was just wanting to eat."

"Is he a better judge than yours truly?"

"Perhaps. One can't underestimate the erotic component of criticism, don't you think?"

"Never."

"Well, Victor's disappeared—is he telling me that I should give up painting?" she said. "Should I?"

"Years ago, a famous artist blessed with late recognition told me, 'Stay in line long enough and eventually you will be served. But never get out of the line.'"

"Should I?"

"Of course not."

"You love me. Victor is more objective," she said, pouring herself another glass of wine. She took a long look into the glass, as if it were a crystal ball revealing her future.

"See anything there?" I asked. "Let me know."

"I have been reading about Eva Hesse," she said. "You knew her, didn't you?"

"Not very well."

"Isn't she one of the artists you're writing about?"

"You have ferret tendencies," I said.

"You seem to have known everyone in your time."

"I may have missed a few, like Poussin and Giotto."

"Seems like no one cared about her work until after she died."

"Well, that's true and not true. Is that what you're worried about, not being known?"

She gave me a studied look. "Would that be wrong?"

"The worry part of it. Look! It's really starting to snow now."

"Please, Charles. Just tell me."

"When I was a kid, I thought everyone cared about the work first and the career second, but I may have been romanticizing it. I tend to do that about artists I love. Sometimes I love the mission as much as the work, love artists who dive—as Melville says."

"That's obvious. That's why I love Eva. Don't you?"

"Yes. And I miss her, though maybe I just miss the intensity of those days." I'd run into Eva at museum and gallery openings and artists' loft parties where everyone danced. I never danced before the mid-1960s; I was always too awkward, too self-conscious. Some of us thought that intellectuals and artists were not supposed to dance or do sports. But then, out of nowhere, we all started dancing, the artists and the writers and the young gallery workers and just anybody in the art world. Sometimes we went to the Dom on the street level of the old Polish National Home on St. Marks Place, in the East Village. We did the twist and made up other moves as we went along. Eva and I sometimes danced together, not well, but we worked at pretending to be happy. We shuffled about, but straining for joy was too much. About midway, we would give up and return to our table, where our friends greeted us with a little salute for our efforts.

Anyway, the point wasn't to dance well, but to go out late, meet friends, and feel a part of American popular culture, which we had snobbishly disdained. Now, we found America vigorous and vital. Europe, far away and exhausted. We thought we owed nothing to it or to the past and, for good or bad, there was freedom in this that Eva fully understood. How could she not have, considering the way she liberated sculpture from its traditional plateaus—taking it off the pedestal and stringing it along wherever she wanted?

I met Eva just after she had separated from a recognized artist, Tom Doyle. Have you ever heard of him? In those openly sexist days, Eva was referred to or thought of solely as his wife. That also explained her nonstatus as an artist. She invited me many times to see her work, usually after we sat down from one of our dance escapades. I always begged off for some reason or another, offering plausible excuses. But at the core, I had little interest in going: She was just a kid with a head full of fancy art school ideas, which, I thought, were not too original, like making art out of nonart.

I'm not sure if most people she invited went to her studio. I did not. I know many who later said they had and that they had loved her work from the start, but I know that is not true.

I thought I heard a car pull into our driveway. I hoped it was the gallery man coming back to offer her a show, but it was just the mail truck making its route. "Well, at least someone other than you has come to see my work. I think you and Victor are my only real fans."

Eva had some fans, like her companion at the time, the sculptor Mike Todd. Mike claimed that there was nothing new to be done in sculpture, that there were only new materials to discover. I guess he and Eva were thinking along the same lines then. No one until Eva had been using rubber and latex and fiberglass instead of metal and stone. Mike was always affectionate with her and she was sweet with him, in a distracted way.

They made fine companions, but not for long. Maybe his polychromatic sculptures of shoe trees were too decorative, too colorful for her and went against the grain of all those gray hanging ropes and felt and those clay mounds of hers. Looking back, she was like nothing else and no one else at the time.

One freezing night in 1966, we three went all the way up to the Nineties in Mike's car to an art-movie house, the Thalia. It was a thrill. None of us had a car and few of our group knew how to drive, being city creatures. I think Eva liked being chauffeured around by Mike. We went to see Godard's *Bande à part.* Afterward, we went to some diner for coffee and rolls—we weren't a drinking crowd then. Eva said she loved the film, especially the dance sequence, which breaks into the film's narrative from out of nowhere—like a flowerpot tossed from a cloud.

I liked the film, too, its freshness; even its dead spots seemed alive. Everything of Godard's broke from the predictable. Of course Eva would love his film.

"Well, if you like the movie so much, why haven't you ever come to my studio?" Eva asked.

That made no sense to me then, but in light of the daring of Godard's film and the belated surprise of finally seeing her art, it makes all the sense in the world. There were stretches in the late 1960s when I was buried in work, and I skipped the dancing and the parties and saw very few people. But one night at an opening at the

Guggenheim, I spied Eva standing alone, apart from the huge crowd. Her head was swathed in a tall turban. I thought that strange, because it wasn't like Eva to be dressed oddly, ostentatiously. Where were the black leggings and the red sweater? We were happy to see each other and kissed. But she seemed subdued, pale and less rosy. I kidded her about the fancy turban. She smiled. "Oh! Charles," she said, with a kind of cheerful sigh, "it's just something I like wearing from time to time."

I didn't know she had undergone an operation for brain cancer, and that in just some few months, I would no longer be able to visit her studio or ever see her again.

"I wish I had known her."

"She seemed so fragile, you know. But she was made of steel."

"What am I made of?"

I waited a moment too long.

"Well, of what, then?"

"Steel, being forged."

She rose and went to the window. Somewhere in the snow was a key to the world.

"Maybe we should go away," she said. "It's disruptive here."

"Is it not quiet enough? Am I not?"

"We are too close to the art world. It's only seventy miles away, but I hear its buzz. It fills my head."

"It fills everyone's head, even in China. It's like the

sirens' song that lures your boat to smash against the rocks."

"Or maybe we're too removed from things. He thinks I should go to New York more often and make the rounds of the galleries, keep abreast of what's happening."

"Why?"

"He thinks my work is too insular."

"Old-fashioned?"

"He didn't say that, exactly."

"Well, what?"

"That it does not have a contemporary look."

"Even if true, so what? Maybe that's your chip."

I saw Victor circling the garden with the paintbrush still between his teeth. "He's back," I said.

She rushed to open the door. "Victor, you've been a bad boy," she said, reaching out to retrieve the paintbrush. He backed away and pricked up his ears.

"Don't chase after him," I said, "or he'll run away and hide it in the woods, where you'll never find it."

She didn't listen. She lunged at him, and he fled. He did not turn when she called his name.

"I'm going to look for him," she said, taking his leash from the doorknob. "I'll be back for dinner. It doesn't matter where we go."

She was out the door and halfway down the garden when she turned about and returned.

"Forget something?"

"Yes."

She kissed me, first on the cheek and then on the mouth, and she brushed back with a tender caress what little hair was still floating on my head.

She was gone. I made myself some lunch from the tatters of the previous day and returned to my study, where she lingered like a cloud in a Tiepolo sky.

I busied myself with nothing and thought about nothing but her. I considered going over into her studio to see the paintings she had shown the gallery man. But that would have been like reading her journal without her invitation. It got dark in the early fall kind of way, from pewter gray to black without a plausible transition. The outside studio lamps went on automatically and spread a yellowish mat over the white carpet of snow. I realized that she had been gone for more than an hour. I phoned. I heard her cell ring in the kitchen. I thought I'd close my eyes for just a few minutes.

The house was empty when I woke. I put on my coat and boots and, ready to search for her and Victor, went down to the kitchen. Outside the window, snow had glazed the lawn in an unbroken silver, except for where she and the dog had left their prints leading up to the studio door. It was dark in there. She was sitting, with Victor at her feet, in her broken-down wicker chair.

Allegory: A Parable

ONCE THE WESTERN WORLD LOOKED ONE WAY, a one-way world, everything pointing back to itself; a tree or the artist's mark representing it on some surface was just a tree staked out there on a plain or hill, or a road simply a road that went from here to there and there to here. These were times when such images gave sufficient pleasure, their presence reminding one of what was out there beyond one's room, and spoke for the way we could transport or fix on a wall our surrounding world. There was no conception then, in this one-way world, of symbol, fable, parable, or allegory: All art was surface and pointed in one direction.

There must have been enough of the world to keep us busy with it in a direct way, not needing to imagine, say, that what we saw was not only the object or scene before our eyes but some idea other than, and in addition to, the object or scene represented.

It was only later that some artists discovered that a tree was also the Rood, Christ's wooden cross, and that a road was also the path of life. They also found, especially after Christianity, that lambs, snakes, and doves doubled for things else. You could make a painting with a single tree on a hill bathed with lambs and a circling luminous dove and, voilà, you at once had a lovely landscape and a tableau portending Christ's Crucifixion on Golgotha. Just remove the dove, put in groves of trees and other creatures, a lion or wolf lying beside a lamb especially, and arrange numerous birds and animals large and small in happy company and, presto: the prelapsarian Garden of Eden. Add a serpent wound tightly on a bough and now it was that same happy garden with a hint of its imminent doom and the Fall.

A landscape—art—could now manifest the natural world and simultaneously imply through its symbols a mythic world, have resonance beyond the image and perhaps awaken in us fears and caution, leaving us to meditate on our origins and our fate: We have arrived in a landscape peopled with symbols, just a short step from the territory of allegory, to which it is neighbor.

Press a symbol and it will jump over into the larger land of allegory, where the landscape echoes with hints of a story or narrative beyond the actual vista.

Take Lorenzetti's fresco *The Effects of Good Government*, a Sienese cityscape of castles and palaces, of the highborn on horses and farmers at their abundant harvest, a portrait of a culture in harmony and order, as there may exist when government is stable and benign. Lorenzetti's painting is a map of place and its medieval time but also sends out whole essays on the conduct of governance that might lead to such secular Edens.

She read these words and others on the matter in books on her barge on the Seine. As it floated, it seemed like a festooned raft in the dark lake where King Arthur had drawn out his magical sword. She read those words again in a quiet park, where she had set up her easel to paint a monument to the triumph of Spring, Winter represented by leaves fallen in postures of despair on the sculpture's base.

This was not the kind of art she made or wanted to make, but she had come to a sorry pass in her work, a grand exhaustion of ideas, she who had had them in proliferation, multiplying like toads in spongy ponds. Allegory seemed exhausted, too. A leftover from the time of knights on wounded missions for the Grail, from a time when everything was an allegory: no bread broken without a thought of that last supper at a long table in spring, no rose springing from a garden without a hint of she who had given immaculate birth and was now the Rose of life and the rosette window shedding a tondo of light on the dark cathedral altar. No thought of dying without seeing a diptych of those who had sinned being led to the burning pits of torture and those who were saved sailing aloft to the Empyrean, where God waited in a white light.

Allegory did not bolt into her mind from nowhere. Not like having a coffee in a park and while looking up at the sky thinking, What ever happened to Allegory? No, she had taken up those books and gave it thought only after seeing a fresco by Puvis de Chavannes in Rouen. *Inter Artes et Naturam*, it was called, and it portrayed various figures in a park by the sea. Men and women and youths in contemplation and study, painters and poets and dreamers in a park of arches and young trees and a fragment of an ancient frieze of Pegasus poised to fly. A land of contentment, as in Lorenzetti's mural, but here the artist muddied the happy scene of the quiet triumph of the arts with some suggestion of sorrow. To the extreme right of the painting and apart from the conclave of artists, a figure of a seated woman, holding an asleep or dead child in her lap. Another woman stands above her. The three forming a triangle of sorrow.

She had seen that painting and had at once dismissed it for its tired sentiment, for its painting of drained figures draped in tissue—as had others of her generation, artists and public alike. But Van Gogh loved it and Gauguin, too, had felt the transcendental shiver it gave. She felt none of that shiver, yet it haunted her, that fresco, and made her think of Poussin's painting *Et in Arcadia Ego* and the four figures reading those words inscribed on a monument or tomb in Arcadia, connecting, as she looked out the window of the train from Rouen to Paris, that forlorn human triangle in Puvis's mural with the idea that even when it is placed in the rearmost wing, Death is at the center of the stage.

Not the sentiment, but the idea that a painting could

extend itself in the mind's time, prolong the duration of art's event, had captured her. She, whose ideas had felt so spent, even now home again in the brightness of New York spring, with all the trucks and traffic on Canal Street, the energy of gears and motors and the stealthy electronic webs netting the atmosphere beneath her eyes and senses. She did not live in a one-way world or in a world that neatly doubled in on itself. Though her life was simple and had purged itself of the superfluous and sometimes even of the necessary, everything she cared for spun with multiplicity, even the pack of chewing gum on the table near her bed.

Little existed without extension and multiplicity, while much of her art, her painting, had held to the idea of art's autonomy—to refer to nothing, to speak with the voice of no discernible person or time or place. (Though she also knew that even in their concealment, all art spoke for those things.)

Not the sentiment of the moralizing of allegory, but its power to sustain time, if not through idea, then through reflection. Something was itself and was something else in addition to it. That became clear to her when she saw in her mirror half her face and hair burnished gold in the morning light, the other half dark in the obscuring shadow caught by the birdcage in her studio window. She considered herself in the old antimonies of light and dark, just human inventions and conventions, and found complexity wanting in the simple dualism.

She was neither light nor dark, nor was the world nor its creations. But, of course, art did not propose such dichotomies, only she did.

"Light and dark with Death waiting in center stage, as well as all the thoughts, including the arguments and ironies against such ideas, are taken up in allegory's silent voice," she heard herself say above the hundred clocks twisting time on their shelves in her studio.

How strange that something so seemingly spent could still be alive—as it was in her, living if only in her thoughts—while buried away for so long in the cellars of tropes and in the dungeons of museums of times dead, of art as useless as armor and pikes. She had left them in a sack, those books and their illustrations, for someone to find on an odd day. But she was haunted by them still, even here, in the New World, at the edge of the century.

Suddenly, all the clocks stopped, very dramatically, she thought, and everywhere. The traffic halted, too. She took her paintings from their racks and tossed them out the window, where they hung in space like postcards fixed on glass. In the stillness of the day, a soft puttering sound and coughing of an engine drifted to her window.

An open barge crowded with people standing and milling about was motoring up the East River and making for the ferry landing. She could see them through her binoculars as they alighted, singly and in pairs. Poussin and Puvis de Chavannes led the procession with chain saws and hammers in hand; Thomas Hart Benton followed, a cornstalk in his belt; Gauguin was there, too, holding a steaming tarbrush aloft, and others she could not identify, and a train of young men and women, some with their bikes, all walking and stopping from time to time to examine the building numbers, searching, it seemed, to find her.

The Phantom Tower

His father, the county doctor, loved him. He read to him even when he returned tired from his rounds—from Miss Biddle, with her gout, and Judge Jackson, with his ever-weakening heart, and all the others in the countryside who needed him. When he turned eight, the doctor gave the boy books for his birthday.

"You have reached the age of reason," the doctor said, "and I will leave you to tell me why I gave you these books in particular." *The History of the Earth* was one, but *Our Unfolding Universe* was the one he loved the best. The boy looked again and again at the large color-plates depicting the world from its earliest days, when the sea churned in a violet light and the sky shone with a gray-blue dullness, as if it were never sure whether it was morning or dusk.

"I think you want me to know, Father, that the world is mysterious and ever-changing."

"And?"

"Beautiful."

"You are a bright boy. Don't let the world dull you."

There was nothing the boy loved more than climbing the ancient oak that rose on the cliff above the sea. He went to his window the moment he woke, and climbed the tree in weather both fair and nasty. He spread himself along the highest branches and took in the changing sky and the moody sea. He could see his cheerful house and the surrounding farms and he knew that wherever he went in life, he would always wish to return there.

When he was ten, the oak tree grew sick—the leaves yellowed, the trunk withered and died. Burly men came to chop it down and cart the wood away. He cried for a whole afternoon and many more afternoons and the mornings that followed, until his father said, "All things die, my son, trees and people, too."

The boy's mother had died soon after he was born, and his father had never remarried. Sometimes, after dinner, his father would withdraw to his book-cluttered study and smoke a wide-bowl briar pipe, and the boy could hear him speaking to someone with his mother's name, but there was no one in the room, only billows of cherry-scented blue smoke.

"Are you talking to my mother?" the boy asked.

"Yes."

"Does she speak to you, even though she is dead?"

"In a way," the doctor said, rising from his chair and hugging his son.

One day, and without fuss, when the boy had turned eighteen, his father died, leaving him the house and the land and a modest but substantial income. The will read: "My son, live, live all you can." He had his father cremated, according to his wishes, and the young man buried the ashes in an urn beside the oak stump. "Ashes," he said, "to think that a life ends in ashes that have no memory."

He left his home soon after and sailed all the seven seas and rode over all the continents by rail and car and bus and by a plane that he himself piloted. He traveled by foot and bike and motorcycle, too, for the intimate feel of the road. He saw towns and cities with their giant buildings pulsating with life. He saw bombed cities that had crumbled into shards of glass and bright steel and saw in everything mutability and transformation: his oak tree into a stump; his father into ashes.

Then he came home. He married a plainspoken woman and they had a son. He loved them both in a respectful way and hid his restlessness and his longing. Longing for what, he did not know.

No one knew who had constructed the tower or had witnessed it being constructed. One day, there was nothing but the green hilly land of his childhood, and the next day, a tower arose where the oak had stood, on the edge of the cliff that overlooked the sea, a tower that pierced the clouds and that surely went beyond.

In his sleep one night, it came to him that he must climb it.

"Who told you to?" his wife asked. "Who told you to

do such a foolish thing? Was it that idiot down the road who eats only plants that face the sun?"

"Not him, no."

"Was it that bald woman who wears a cardboard sign saying that the world is doomed to suffocate itself?"

"Not her, either," he said.

"Then who?"

"The tower itself."

"It spoke to you, the tower?"

"In my sleep."

"Are you sure it was not a burning bush," she asked, "or a talking snake?"

"The tower. And I'm going to climb to its top."

"Maybe there's a beanstalk and a giant up there, Dad," his ten-year-old son said.

"Maybe Jack will be there, too, my son. I will tell him you said hello."

She walked him to the door of their cottage and gave him a thermos of water and a blue sweater she had knit for his birthday. "I will have dinner ready, fool," she said, kissing him on each cheek.

It took him hours to climb to the first tier of the tower. He rested there and took in the view. There was his teacher's house, where she lived with two yellow dogs and a tall woman with one arm; there was the volunteer fire station where his father had played chess with the chief, an atheist who prayed when the alarm sounded; there was Mary Cook's saltbox of a house with its sugar white clapboards and slanted chimney. She was his first love and got married when he was away on his travels.

"Come home! Come home!" his wife shouted to him from far below, from the lower rungs.

"Not yet," he said, climbing higher.

She shouted again, but he cupped his ear and waved to her as if to say, Don't worry yourself; I will be home one day. He wondered if he had conveyed the message with his wave.

It was bracing, the land with the screen of the sky and the iron rungs each with their thickness and certainty. He was sure they would never give way under his foot or break under the grasp of his hand as he reached above and pulled himself higher and higher toward the faraway turret that capped the tower.

He saw the rivers and valleys, forests laced with streams. He felt the chill of snowcapped mountains just yards from his feet. When he arrived at the next tier, he felt himself lighter and, dare he say, younger, as if the weight of the years and loss had vanished.

By his second day of climbing, he had forgotten hunger and thirst and sleep. But he had not forgotten his wife and son and their cozy home always smelling of cinnamon and baking bread. He paused to picture them.

A hot-air balloon with a basket carrying a man drifted up alongside him. "Dad, time to come home," the man said.

The man looked too old to be the boy he had left behind only days ago, and he said, "Who has sent you?"

"We who love you, Dad. Come back to earth; come back to terra firma, Dad, and to what loves you."

"I want to reach the top first and see what is to be seen from it," he said, at last recognizing his son's features.

"And to what you love, Dad," he added as the balloon suddenly descended in a powerful downdraft.

What did he love, or had he ever loved, on earth? The giant oak tree of his youth that he climbed on summer days to look out to the sea in the distance. The sea that one day he had come to know like a brother of another time. His father and the billowing smoke of his father's pipe in the room of his loneliness.

The call to return home and to those who loved him was strong, but the drive to continue was stronger. "Inexorable," he said, as if to explain the force that propelled him.

The earth far below sent up waves of ominous heat, and the rivers looked like threads of blood; the ocean had congealed into a mirrorlike sheet, the winds having sanded it to a high, dead shine, although here and there a toylike ship broke the ocean's uniform skin, rising like a pustule.

"Beautiful," he said, "beautiful, the world." He had said the same at the Ganges, when he watched the dead fuel the wooden pyres and their bones and ashes scattered into the sacred river.

When he was a boy, he had asked his father, "What is the world made of?" "Made of nothing and is nothing," his father had replied.

He knew that was not true, that the world was made of oceans and mountains and glorious trees, like the old oak he had loved.

"Then what is it that we see and touch, Father?"

"A phantom, my son."

He began to despair that there was no end to his climb; the higher he reached, the farther the top. It struck him, too, that he was the only one climbing the tower; he looked below and saw no one, and no one above, either. But as he went higher, he thought he had spied someone in the upper reaches, only to find a golden condor perched on a rung. It spoke to him: "Only a bit more," the bird said in the reassuring voice of his father, "and it is done." Then he spread his enormous golden wings and disappeared into the sky.

When he stepped onto the final tier, it was carpeted with his childhood books, and scattered about, the six missing crayons from his classroom desk, and his comb, with all its tines, which had dropped from his pocket in a fight on his way to school. He recognized there, too, resting on its side, his father's briar pipe. He picked it up and sat down.

Delacroix in Love

I WOKE UP IN THE MORNING speaking French and found that Pascal had come back, his left ear bent like a furry maple leaf. I tried to straighten it, but he pinched me with his needle teeth. He had been gone for over two weeks. I had plastered everywhere his photo and my number and a promise of a reward, but no one ever called.

At first, my French was just a few phrases sliced into the English.

"Such a beautiful day now that Pascal's back home," I said over breakfast to my still sleepy wife, "*n'est-ce pas?*"

"I told you he'd be back," my wife said.

"*Oui, c'est ça.*"

"What's with the frog talk all of a sudden?"

"*Je sais pas,*" I said with a Gallic shrug of the shoulders.

"It's annoying. Quit it."

The odd thing was that I had never studied French or been to France or any francophone country. I regularly watched French movies at one of the few remaining art houses in the city but never bothered to join the actors' voices with the subtitles, and thus I learned nothing of how to speak in that sex-soaked language where a noun sounds like a flirtation. I liked French, and I also enjoyed hearing Italian and Spanish and German, but I did not wake up one morning speaking them.

My wife had left me some months ago to live with a man who owned a small but successful taxi fleet that sped through the fancier regions of the Hamptons. I had met him a few times at parties and benefits under summer tents. I liked his red pants and tasseled moccasins and that he said, "If you ever need a cab, use my name with the dispatcher."

"He just got divorced," my wife whispered at the punch bowl after he had turned to a woman who called out the man's name in capitals. "He's interested in buying one of your paintings. I told him they were great." I was happy when she left me and was unhappy when she returned, each feeling canceling out the other, so I was left neither happy nor unhappy, but with a strange sense of benign resignation.

⁂

Every other Sunday, Delacroix put aside his work, spruced up, and went to the Gare Montparnasse to meet the woman he loved. The little train from Auvers-sur-Oise always deposited her on time, and he was always there waiting for her on time.

"Your regularity amazes me. If I didn't know you

were such a great artist, I would have taken you for an accountant or a bureaucrat."

"I take this as a great compliment," he said. "I had always wanted to be a lawyer and arrange wills and divorces, but my parents forced me to become an artist."

The lovers often strolled about the Luxembourg Garden and lunched nearby, *sur la terrace*, if the weather allowed. By late afternoon they were drinking mint tea at his apartment, the cup packed with dark leaves and clotted with sugar, the way it was prepared in Morocco, he told her. They eventually made their way to his lumpy bed, where they lingered until Sunday evening. On Monday morning, she took the train back to her unhappy mother. They were in love and would marry when he had sufficient income to provide for them both and for another or two, should they be so blessed. She was twenty-three, he forty-four. And she would wait.

Sometimes they spent their Sunday afternoons with his closest friend, Charles Soulier, a surgeon, whom Delacroix had known since university days. The three might take a train as far as Saint-Cloud and, in the ancient park of old oak trees, picnic under the cobalt sky. There, on a carpet piled with wine bottles and a wicker basket of fruit and cheeses and a roasted chicken, Charles lamented that he found medicine boring and his wealthy patients and their phantom ills beyond boring, and that he wished he could live as interestingly as did his friend and, like him, go off to Morocco and paint its exotic people, still untouched by violent machines and corrupting progress.

She laughed. "Do you think Eugène has an interesting life? Until I met him, I thought artists were wild and lived in cafés and brothels when they were not dabbling with paint."

"It's the doctor here who has what you imagine the artist's life," Delacroix said. "He carves up people in the morning, sleeps all day, and has half the women in Paris charging his bed at night."

"You call that a life?" the doctor said. "If only one day I could meet a woman as vivid and beautiful as you, Clothilde."

"Search for a woman with whom you can have happiness in your life," Clothilde advised.

"I would find happiness if you had a twin."

❖

"I want to write a book on artists and their travels," I said, my mind filled with Delacroix's letters, and his journals, which I thought were as moving as his paintings.

"Save your time for painting," my wife said. "There are hundreds of books like that."

"I'm sure. But I want to sort out the art that is an elevated travelogue from that which is pure art."

"Now there's something, a book that will explain what pure art is."

"Think of it! Before photography, artists always went

to faraway places to market exotic scenes to people back home—Delacroix's Morocco paintings, for example."

"Exotic pornography," she said. "Half-naked slave girls in harems. I'm sure that sold like hotcakes in Delacroix's time."

"Why do hotcakes sell so well?"

"It's just an expression."

"Sure, but what is a hotcake?"

When I looked up, she was gone. But Pascal had leapt to the table and was eating a slice of smoked salmon right off the plate. My wife never would have allowed that, but he knew I was a sucker for all his desires.

"What do you think of my idea, Pascal? I know you were listening."

He curled himself on the table and let out a fishy yawn. I noticed that in speaking with Pascal, I spoke English, his only language.

"All those artists on the move, Pascal. Imagine what a schlep it was for Gauguin to get to Tahiti, or Delacroix to Morocco. Makes you wonder. Of course, there are the stay-at-homes, Monet and his garden, Pollock and his paint-splattered floor in the Springs. See what I mean, Pascal? They didn't have to travel an inch from home."

I heard my wife rumbling upstairs in her bedroom and wondered if she was unpacking or packing to leave again. She appeared minutes later.

"Are you ever going to speak to me in English?" She was in blue shorts and a fetching red halter; her cork-soled platform shoes sported blueberries on the straps tied above her ankles. I looked at her for a full long minute. She smiled.

"*Peut-être,*" I said in what I thought was a flirty way.

"Your cat peed in my bed while I was gone."

"He must have been claiming it as his after you left," I wrote in my notebook as she read over my shoulder.

"I invited some people to come over to see your paintings, so please stop fooling around with the French stuff."

"*D'accord.*"

The French windows opened to the patio, which stopped at a pool nestled against a wooden fence. Beyond the fence were scrub bushes and trees and a path that lead to the ocean. I could hear the ocean at night and was grateful I was on land. I hated travel by sea; hated it by land or air, *en plus.*

I had named him when he was still in his litter. I knew right away we were made to be friends. And later, when he was just some months old, I was proved right when he started his long sits by the bay window that fronted the open sky. I knew that, like me, he was a daydreamer and not a voyager. Hence, I named him after the French philosopher who asked God to give him the patience to sit.

"It's so pretentious to call a cat Pascal," my wife had said. "It embarrasses me. What's wrong with Tom, or Tiger, or Jake?"

She addressed him by all of those names. He gave her his yawn of indifference and retreated to me. It was after that that he began his peregrinations. Or maybe he had sat long enough and thought to see a bit of the world before he died.

I once got a call from the movie house in Southampton, saying that after the last show, when they were cleaning up, they had found Pascal sleeping in the rear with a dead mouse between his teeth. How had he gotten there, a walk of twelve miles from my house?

He once took to the road, my little hitchhiker, and was picked up by a couple on their way to Florida who thought that he had been abandoned by summer people. They called me a week after when they discovered his name tag buried under his burr- and leaf-coated neck. I had to fly to Naples, Florida, and rent a car to take him home. He was silent the entire twenty-one-hour drive back, even though I spoke to him in the most affectionate way.

I walked to my studio and examined the paintings hanging along the walls: sailboats in a race, their spinnakers billowing; fishing boats in a high sea cast in a silvery, moon-thick sky. I sold well at the less known, local galleries and as far afield as Martha's Vineyard and Kent, Connecticut. For a time, I painted the show horses of people who wanted their equine world immortalized. I was always in demand and could have painted horses until I died and I would have died with a plus in my estate. But the sea and its implied adventures, its high romance is what I went for and stayed with, as long as I did not have to board a watery craft.

Over the years, I had made friends with famous artists in an area known for famous artists. I was never anxious about their fame or that my work was in radical contrast to theirs. I was pleased with what I did and that was all that mattered to me or all that I let matter. I had been asked many times by my artist friends to show them my work, but I was too shy to invite them to my studio until one said, "Nicolas, let your friends see who you are."

I did. And there was always a little chill after that whenever we met at dinner parties. "Nicolas is trying to drag painting back to the nineteenth century," I had heard that one of them had said.

Pascal came in and circled my ankles three times and let out a little cry of hello. I lifted him into my arms and walked him about the studio. He had always been my most appreciative audience.

"Pascal," I said. "Are you going to leave me again?"

The moment I said that, I realized that for him, the unknown streets he prowled were his oasis and his desert sands. The females he met in dark alleyways were his mobile harem, for him to choose among day or night. In retrieving him from his wanderings time and time again, what adventures had I deprived him of?

I heard voices and, sure enough, it was my wife and

her guests. The man was wearing green pants and red tasseled moccasins and a plaid shirt open at his sun-tanned, gray-haired chest; the woman with him had the face of a grilled wallet.

"I need something for my dining room," he said after we shook hands, "and I don't want something trendy that anyone can get at Gagosian or Zwirner."

"*Oui, je comprends.*"

"Is your husband French?" she asked.

"He lived in France a long time," my wife said, "and sometimes he lapses into the language."

He stopped before a painting of a schooner at dusk turning in the wind and a white-capped sea. The last rays of the sun gleamed off the stern.

"There is much melancholy here," he said. "A wistfulness."

"*Merci,*" I said, touched.

"You are the schooner at its last light, *n'est-ce pas?*"

"*Justement,*" I said. "*Vous avez tout compris.*"

With my painting under his arm, he took me aside as they were leaving and said, "Your wife still loves you. She just needed a fling."

Once he was back from Morocco, Delacroix ceased his travels. Some of his very few friends noticed that ever since his return from "the land of the sun," as he called Morocco, he had grown ever more reclusive. He invented absurd excuses to avoid accepting dinner invitations—my shoes walked off during the night—but the invitations grew with his increasing fame. He ate alone, one meal a day in the early evening, and took to his bed at an hour when others were stirring to leave their houses for a party or a dinner with friends. To a close friend, who had lamented that she longed to see him, Delacroix wrote, "Passion cannot give one lasting well-being. That lies only within oneself. The only real satisfaction I feel is with work." The friend was surprised by these words, as she had only asked Delacroix to dine with her and her husband before the month was out. And she was even more surprised when she read "When a man has lost love, he has lost everything."

No one knew what had caused the change in him; that secret, Delacroix kept to himself.

In his months away in Morocco, the call to prayer from the mosques that reached to the clouds, the steeds and their riders racing between the beach's edge and the ocean's spume, the round women and their soft eyes, the gardens of jasmine dizzying the air, all had impregnated him, but they had not covered the space where Clothide lived.

They had met a week after he returned from Tangier and took their walk in the Luxembourg Garden and lunched at their favorite café, went to his apartment and drank mint tea and sank into his lumpy bed. But something had changed. She cried at the train station when he came to meet her, she teared up during their garden walk and at lunch, and she wept in bed. At first, he had thought that the emotion of seeing him after his long absence had brought on all these tears, and he was flattered at the salty evidence that she loved him so greatly. He himself looked at her with moist, adoring eyes.

At breakfast the next morning, more of the same. Until he asked, "My dear, what is the matter?"

"It was not his fault," she said. "Nor mine. It was that we both missed you so much."

It was rare to read a letter with such dignity and sadness, I thought after reading it twice. I read it aloud to Pascal the third time while he was on my lap, and he feigned some interest before he went to sleep. It was to Delacroix's dearest friend, Charles Soulier, whom he now addressed in the formal *vous.*

"You treated as a passing moment, without repercussion, what for me completely had filled my heart and soul." He added, "Fabricate for our friends a reason why we no longer see each other." I wonder what he wrote or said to Clothide, whom he never saw again.

He caught colds, and many of his letters refer to his long stays in bed. He poured his ailments into his correspondence and, as he grew older, his letters grew ever more warm and feelingful and, at points, almost confessional, as if their distance allowed him the safety to open his heart. To George Sand, he wrote, "Let us love one another, then, with or without fame. It's not your fame I love, it's you."

His letters kept him warm and his paintings kept him active, but, for all that, he spent the rest of his life in bed, alone.

❖

My wife was by the pool, a drink in hand. She smiled. She raised her glass in a salute of celebration. "I knew he would like your paintings."

"*Oui, il me semble qu'on a le même goût.*"

I moved toward the house and then toward the studio and then went toward the garage and then back to the studio, where I studied my paintings. I did not hate them and I did not love them, but they had left me. They had gone from me along with English, my own language, and with the painting under the arm of my wife's lover.

What if I left, as had Pascal so many times, without a word or a sign, and took the first plane to anywhere and just lived, whatever that meant? Now that I spoke French, why not live in Paris, where I could sit in a café packed with poets and artists and their models, who forever loved them, even committing suicide after their deaths? I could paint the Seine and Notre-Dame with its rosette window; I could paint the Luxembourg Garden; I could paint the Paris that I had known only in the movies and in photographs and bring the city to a life that it had never before known. I could take Pascal with me. He could learn French easily and a new universe would open up to him, to us.

I went to get Pascal's travel box in the attic. It was dusty. As soon as he saw it, he fled under my bed. It was a struggle to extract him, but I finally won and urged him into the cage. I put the box on the seat beside me and drove through town to where I had once found him basking under a staircase that led to the beach. He had looked disappointed, but let me take him home; he had been at large only two weeks but had already assumed a grizzled, feral look of vast independence. I opened the box; he stalked away, looked about, and, on his own volition, slid back in.

Then I hit on a new idea. I drove to the East Hampton train station and let him out on the platform. I removed and pocketed his name tag. I picked him up and gave him a hug and a kiss that he managed to avoid. But once again when on the ground, he snuggled up close until the westbound train arrived with great self-importance. Pascal entered, turned about to face me, and yawned as the train slid shut its doors.

Nine Flowers

—1—

Except for three faded cloth roses in a chipped glass vase on my mother's night table, roses my father had given her during their courtship in the darkest days of the Great Depression, there were no flowers in my home.

When I was ten, I was faced with roses both red and white. The white ones, my mother said, expressed special sympathy for the bereft, and they were heaped alongside my young cousin's open coffin in a funeral parlor in the upper Bronx.

I shied away from flowers, connecting them with the waxy faces of corpses stiff in polished wooden boxes. Only later, in my early teenage years, when I first fell in love, did I lose my dread of flowers and come to love them and their mystery.

—2—

That spring of '73, I lunched alone every day at La Carbonara in the Campo de' Fiori. Salome, the owner and my longtime friend, would sometimes come by and sit at my table and ask about America. She was at the lean end of sixty and had never left Rome; she wanted to see America before she died.

"Is it worth going?" she asked.

"Salome, if I still had an apartment overlooking this square, and every day I could see the flower carts and hear the vendors cry out the names of their specialties—roses, irises, lilies, violets—I would never leave to go to America or to any other place on this Earth."

"Yes," Salome said. "I know you would have stayed here forever if she had not left you."

"She is rare," I said.

–3–

Henry Adams wrote a small book about the famous medieval cathedral at Chartres. He expatiated on its being the central image of piety, transcending all classes of the Christian world. Knight and serf were cohorts under its vaulted roof. He was particularly struck by the cathedral's giant rose window, finding divinity in its rosy glow.

My stomach hurt from some bad food I had eaten before we drove to Chartres. I had come to see the famous cathedral because of Adams, because his prose had convinced me the trip would be worth it. She had come along to please me.

"Isn't that what companions do, try to make life

agreeable for each other?" she said, rolling down the car window.

"You could have stayed at the hotel. I wouldn't have minded."

"You would have," she said. "In any case, all you had to say was 'Thank you for coming with me.'"

"Thank you for coming with me."

On our way, we stopped at a roadside flower stall and spotted a pot of roses still fragrant with the scent of first morning light.

"These," she said to the young man at the stand.

"Maybe not those. I have better," he said, offering her a bouquet of irises.

She looked at me, then him, saying, "The roses are my desire."

"A boy brought them to me this morning. He had taken them from a nearby cemetery. I scolded him. But I could see he was poor, and I paid him."

"Give me seven," she said, pointing to the ones with the darkest hue.

"Tainted by death," I thought to say, but did not.

He shrugged. "As you like. I hope they bring you good fortune."

Back in the car, she kept the flowers on her lap.

"I could hide in these flowers. I could hold them to me against the world," she said.

At first, it seemed very dark inside the cathedral. Cool and dark, while outside was burning and bright. It was empty except for us, which surprised me, considering its vast reputation.

We sat quietly, and gradually we became accustomed to the darkness; we soon realized it was not dark at all but that we were in a light that was neither day nor night. There was no inside or outside, but only a center, whose solar light, as it filtered through the rose window, had transformed itself into spirit.

"What do you think?" she asked. "Is this the trick that kept the medieval world in a stupor of belief?"

"It could turn a Marxist around, even."

"Don't exaggerate."

"An atheist, then."

We drove back without stopping. And we said nothing and saw nothing but the road ahead. Somewhere along the way, we knew we would now live forever in the immortal aura of that rosy window. We said we would live forever and forever for each other, we said.

—4—

When I was a boy, I often saw veterans of the Great War selling paper poppies on the street corners. My mother always bought three and paid triple the asking price of a nickel and repeated her thank-you with the warmest of smiles.

There was always something wrong with these men. One was blind and wearing an old-fashioned khaki uniform with puttees; his voice trembled when he spoke.

Another had an empty sleeve for an arm and a leather patch masking one side of his face—the other side was grilled meat. He darkened my dreams for weeks, even after my mother had assured me that he was a brave man and a hero and deserved my admiration.

"I never want to be a hero, then," I said.

–5–

Even before the cannon went off marking the Ramadan fast, the streets went empty and only the Café de Paris had some few people drinking pots of mint tea beside us on the terrace. A silence came from nowhere and surrounded us and made everything still until the sparrows landed in the jasmine trees and sat on the empty café tables and began their besotted serenade. A scent of jasmine floated in the Tangier air and covered the world. The sparrows took in its sweet aroma and suddenly ceased their ecstatic chippering and froze in place, like fists of feathered coal.

She was made of jasmine, I told her. Her voice, too. Her words came to me pillowed on jasmine petals. She put her jasmine hand on mine.

–6–

"I got your flowers this morning, thank you. They're very pretty."

"Oh!"

"Well, it was the thought anyway, I suppose."

"Don't you like roses?"

"Sure, you know I do. So I was surprised you didn't send me roses."

"Of course I did. That's what I ordered on the phone."

"That's funny, they brought me a bunch of wilting violets."

"I can't believe they could be so stupid. Let me call them."

"Don't bother, unless you want to."

"Anyway, why would you ever think I would send you violets?"

"To remind me that I'm a shrinking violet."

"That's silly."

"That's what you called me once. Don't you remember?"

"Because when we started dating, you wouldn't let me kiss you, and you pulled away."

"'What are you,' you said, 'a shrinking violet?'"

"You don't shrink now."

"Why? Am I too clinging?"

"Not at all clinging."

"Like a clinging vine, like a flowering clematis, right?"

"I'm going to call the flower shop."

"Don't bother."

"Okay, I won't."

—7—

The revolution was over and the victors were cleaning house. A thousand revolutionaries and their allies were gathered in a great hall, waiting to be addressed by the party leader.

The leader thanked his supporters in the name of the revolution and, to those still on the political fence, he said, "Let a hundred flowers grow."

I imagined those flowers in a field as far as the horizon, hundreds all in harmony, gently contending for soil and air and sun, all waiting for the rain, all wanting to live. And all being let to live in their variety, and with no one flower allowed to overshadow and to stunt the growth of the others.

"Now," the leader continued, "I invite you to speak openly and without fear of retribution about whatever disagreements exist within and outside our party. Tell us how to bring our revolution forward and with productive comradeship." Those assembled cheered and applauded for a full fifteen minutes, and a great wave of euphoria filled the hall.

Over the next several weeks, hundreds of letters came to the leader. Some maintained that the revolution had gone too far and too fast; some proposed that the leadership be voted upon in a free election; some denounced the party itself for having assumed the very privileges of the class it had recently overthrown.

Within a year, all those who had written letters had disappeared.

We woke one morning and I looked out our window and saw a field stretching as far as the horizon. On the ground, the chopped heads of hundreds of flowers, each rotting in its own way, under a scorching sun. I turned to her and said, "Let's return to bed, my love, and let's never again speak or think of flowers."

–8–

Vincent loved flowers, especially sunflowers thick and ready to burst with seed and listing with heavy, torpid heads. In Arles, he painted them all day as he and they sweltered in the sun. At night, they nearly fell off the canvas in their sleepy weight.

He loved sunflowers and thought them little pieces of the sun come to visit Earth. He loved Arles, their home, even though the flowers there exploded in his head and drove him mad, until he hurt himself.

All the same, whenever he felt the chill of being alive, of being a man drifting in the cold ocean of stars, he stood before his sunflower paintings for warmth.

He loved irises more than any other flower in the world, their mineral blue like a saint's robe in a Giotto painting. He painted irises as they swam tightly together in the little garden of the clinic at Saint-Rémy, where he was striving to become healthy after his breakdown in Arles. Their blueness calmed him, stopped him from trembling.

I took the train from Paris to Auvers-sur-Oise and went directly to the cemetery where Vincent and his beloved brother were buried side by side. I had made the same pilgrimage twice before and had even thought I might live there for a year or two. Or maybe at the end, I'd find a plot for myself in the same cemetery as Vincent's, so that I would never be far from him.

I had thought first to bring sunflowers to his grave and then I thought a bouquet of irises might be better—in case he was disquieted. But in Paris, in August, there were no sunflowers at the market and no irises, either. I took with me instead the three paper poppies I carry on my travels as a charm to make me brave. I placed two at Vincent's headstone, and the third at his brother's.

–9–

"I had a little apartment overlooking the Campo de' Fiori," she said. "That was before I met you."

"The same apartment where we lived together?"

"No. I would never live with a man in an apartment where I had lived with another man. Don't you know me? I had several suitors then. What single woman, a foreigner in Rome, does not? You don't even have to be very pretty."

"That leaves you out, then, because you are not at all pretty."

"Thank you."

"You are more than pretty. You're rare."

She smiled, but it was a sign of punctuation rather than of favor.

"One of these suitors was a handsome Sicilian,

twenty-two or -three. Slender and with black hair down to his shoulders. So black that the top of his head disappeared in the night. He always wore a suit, white shirt open at the collar, and his black shoes bounced light. He spoke perfect English."

"A handsome English-speaking Sicilian. I suppose he was rich, too."

"Old money and a title."

"Please tell me the point of this story."

"Jealous?"

"Of course."

"You know, in life, there is always someone more handsome than you. Or richer or taller or more interesting or more talented, more sexy."

"I'm sure. But in your case, there is no one more anything than you, ever."

Another smile, but warmer this time.

"He sent me red roses. A dozen at a time. Three or four times or more over the course of the day, every day."

"Where did you have the room?"

"This went on for weeks. Sometimes I'd see him standing beside one of the flower carts below me in the square. He wore a rose in his lapel that he touched when he bowed. Just to make sure that I understood."

"A rose between his teeth, as well?"

"I wanted to tell him, 'You could have had me weeks ago and now you're crushing me with flowers.' I wanted to escape."

"Did you?"

"He didn't know that an even dozen of roses is vulgar. What kind of aristocrat doesn't know that? Even you know that."

"Even I."

"I liked from the start that you sent me only nine. Don't ever send me more than nine."

"Only nine. And never white."

The Garden Party

"WHAT I LIKE MOST IN ART IS DISQUIETUDE," I said, my hand reaching for the martini pitcher.

"Expatiate on this theme later, after the party. Or maybe never," Alice said. "And please get dressed."

We were in the garden, by the pool, the patio umbrella casting a bronze shadow over me in the milky sun.

"I'm dressed."

"Pajamas is not what I had in mind," she said, slyly moving the pitcher out of my reach.

Behind me, a white two-story house, mine and hers. Similar houses of varying size and manifest affluence stretched in line, row after row, to a vanishing point. A flower garden in luxuriant bloom—our gardener saw to that. A kidney-shaped pool, where a giant orange rabbit spun slowly in a delicate breeze.

"And get rid of the rabbit. It's not funny."

"It's meant to hit a disquieting note, a discordant tone, like the unexpected that I love in art, as I mentioned a moment ago."

"Yes, and as you have mentioned for a decade. You

should never have a martini before guests arrive. It encourages the pontifical in you."

"I'm not in the mood for a party. Phone everyone and say I'm sick. Chills and cough and shakes. A whiff of the bubonic."

I was happy sitting with my view of Main Street in the near distance, and beyond that the shopping mall on a hill, and beyond that a highway, choked with cars and trucks, bordered by a forest of young trees gasping for air.

"You call," Alice said.

"Then who's going to believe I'm sick? Who's coming anyway?"

"The usual. Mary Holiday and her husband, the doctor; the bankers, Jesse and his brother Frank; Eric Armstrong and his fiancée, Honey Flakes McBride, the former golf pro you flirt with; Charles Coverdale, the creep who sold you the fake Rolex. Then there's the indicted mortgage broker, George le Blanc, and the defrocked missionary, Padre Paul."

"That's it?"

"Not at all, the mayor and the sheriff; the high school principal and his wife, the town slut; the retired army private; our indicted assemblyman; and everyone from my firm I need to suck up to."

A deer, followed by a bear, a fox, a raccoon, and a bobcat, all took their time strolling before us. The bear turned and, in the most cavalier, affronting way, tossed a shredded bag of pretzels into the pool. I quickly got distracted. "Do you smell smoke?" I asked, rising from my chaise longue.

"Of course! Just turn your head. Jack and Jan's house is on fire."

"Again?"

Fire engines drew up with sirens and horns blasting. Firemen dragged hoses, quivering like flattened pythons, into the garden, and milled before the burning house. They chattered, smoked cigarettes, played cards, and shot dice while Jack and Jan stood by, studying the fire. I waved and they waved back, smiling.

"Do you think the fire will spread to us?" Alice asked.

"Not a chance," I said. "Unless the wind blows this way."

The fire chief called over the fence. "Do you mind if we pail some water from your pool?"

"Be my guest," I said.

"Be our guest," Alice added.

"Thanks for the *aqua,* our pool's kaput," Jan said, coming to visit.

"Don't forget to come by later," Alice said. "It's just us and the old gang."

"And invite anyone you like," I said. "By the way, your porch is ablaze."

"And they claim it's fire-resistant!" Jack said.

"It's just cheap pressed wood. I told you so," Jan said, breathing out a plume of smoke. "My husband's always looking for bargains," she added, turning to the fire chief and the six handsome young firemen carrying metal pails.

"Please don't throw your cigarettes in the pool," my wife asked the firemen in what I thought was a seductive voice.

"Let's get started, boys," the chief said. The men lined up, filled their pails, and, in a file, took turns splashing water on the burning house.

"The fire's traveling to your second floor," Alice said.

"It's a crisp and orderly fire," I added.

"Yes, it's a fire with precision, which I prefer to the chaos of the fireplace," Jan said, looking exceptionally youthful.

"So few people appreciate nuance," my wife said. "That's why we cherish you as neighbors."

"I was saying to Alice just before you came how much I like the discordant in art."

"I couldn't agree more," Jan said. "Art must be discordant or be nothing at all."

"But not stridently or flamboyantly so, as with surrealism, and its obvious and conventional gimmicks," Jack added.

"I agree wholly, Jack. And quietude must underline and foil the discord," I said, pleased with myself.

Just then my wife, shielding her eyes from the blaze, said, "Don't your in-laws live in the second story?"

"Why, yes, what a good memory you have," Jack said.

"But those two are never going to leave," Jan noted. "Once they're glued to their game shows, they stay put, earthquake or tornado or fire, no matter what."

"In my younger days, I used to like *Wheel of Fortune*," the fire chief said. "There was also one with different doors. Some had prizes behind them and you had to guess which door."

"Why don't you come by later for drinks and the barbecue," Alice told the fire chief, "and the boys, too, of course."

"Love to, but there's a giant conflagration on the other side of town that needs attending to."

"Do you have enough pails, Chief?" Jan asked. "We have a few in the garage we can lend you."

"The problem's not the pails. It's the pools. They have almost no pools over in that section of town."

"How some people live!" Jan exclaimed. "I myself value a pool above a kitchen. After all, there's always takeout. But I suppose not everyone feels that way."

I wanted to tell them about a painting, in line of what we had been discussing earlier. But then Jan said, "It's getting really warm out here. May we have something to drink?"

I was appalled by my lack of hospitality and rattled the ice cubes in the shaker. With apologies, I made a new batch of martinis and poured all around. Within a few minutes, Jack said, "This is great, Ted. Even minus the olives, you make a perfect martini."

A whine, a whizzing, and a popping overhead, red, white, and blue flares burst in the sky. A parade of cars, trucks, floats with banners of the American Legion, the Elks, the Veterans of Foreign Wars, White's Apothecary flowed along Main Street, followed by a marching band blasting John Philip Sousa.

"What is it anyway, the Fourth, or Memorial Day, or Thanksgiving?" Jack asked, waving away the smoke veiling the air about us.

"It's one of those days," Jan said, her hair frizzing in the fire's heat. "Anyway, it's getting too hot here. Mind if we go over and sit in your pool?"

"That's a good, idea," Alice said; "let's all go." But at that moment, a van arrived, crushing the flower beds and indenting the grass. "Oh! Finally," Alice cried. "I thought they'd never show."

The caterers quickly set up ten round tables and chairs and umbrellas and two wet bars.

"Where's the food?" Alice asked in a modulated panic.

Another van skidded to a stop; the driver emerged waving a paper. Four men in aprons hauled out and spread on the grass five gutted pigs, six sides of beef, five fifty-pound plastic bags of chopped meat, eight plucked chickens, headless but alive.

"Sign the receipt," the driver said.

"What about the buns and the condiments?"

"What about the beverages?" I called out.

"The delivery truck turned over on Utopia Parkway, and now it's a river of sodas and booze," the driver said.

"Where," Alice asked, "are the bartenders and the waitstaff? They're already late!"

"Twelve have Ebola and two have gone to see the fireworks. Sign," the driver said, thrusting the pen toward Alice's face.

"Not in this lifetime."

The driver nodded to the four men who, shouldering the bags of meat, made their way to the pool.

"Give me the pen," Alice said, "but forget the tip."

"We'd better get going," the chief said, pointing to the smoke-choked sky. "Before we know it, the whole town will go up."

"Can we go with you?" Jan and Jack called out, sunk to their necks in the pool.

"Why not, I know how you kids love a fire."

"Come back soon," I shouted, waving to the departing fire truck, its sirens overriding my voice.

"I'm so glad they left," I said. "There's no serious conversation in them, nothing beyond a few minutes. I was about to talk about an old master painting I love, a man walking in a serene landscape and quiet sky. You couldn't ask for a nicer day. But when you look up close, you see a giant snake waiting, unseen in the man's path."

"Have you noticed," Alice asked, before I could continue, "that our house's caught fire?"

"Our neighbors' houses, as well," I said, pointing out

the obvious. House after house burning in succession, like a row of falling dominoes. Sparrows dropped from the sky like charred rocks.

"What's the point of ever making plans?" Alice said glumly.

Pointing to the singed, soot-covered people, stumbling their way toward us, I said, "Look, our guests are arriving."

The Restaurant. The Concert. The Bar. The Bed. *Le Petit Déjeuner.*

Central Park spread outside the window, the evening transforming shrubs and trees and the Egyptian obelisk into silhouettes. Snow drifted down flake by flake and two hit the window, each melting into another state. When we die, don't we also go into another state?

I started to give voice to this ancient question, but, turning from the window, Marie spoke first. "You live your life and then, bang, suddenly it's all looking back."

"Is it the snow outside that makes you think this now?"

"No, it's this restaurant. Everyone's old and every last one is regretting what they've left undone and where they went wrong."

"Everything I've done is wrong, so I don't really dwell on it. I'd rather sit here and dwell on you."

"Dwell away," she said. "Still, this is the most boring restaurant in the whole world. No wonder it suits you."

"I like that it's beige and tame."

"You just summed up your taste in art, buddy," she said, pointing—rudely, I thought—her salad fork at me.

"I like all kinds of art and all kinds of women, except rude ones with spears."

"Do you like them when they are overripe like old pears with brown bruises?"

As if not having heard her, I said, "And dessert? What appeals to you?"

"Hemlock, please."

"Or maybe an espresso, if they've run out?"

"Natch."

"What's with the argot?"

Luis, the waiter, who had known us a long time, came by to take our dessert order, adding, "You have twenty-five minutes to get down to the concert."

I thanked him and she thanked him and I thanked him again.

"You mean 'What's with the slang?' *Argot* means specialist language, like the kind criminals use," she said.

"I'm hip to the criminal argot," I said. "Like shiv or screw or gator tossing the salad."

"I swoon," she said in a sexy whisper, "when you make like a street urchin from Hell's Kitchen."

"That dates you," I said. "Hell's Kitchen's gone upscale."

"You're an urchin anyway. But with friendly spines and a soft shell and a mushy middle." She showed a thread of a smile, as when she won a round at bridge.

"You know, my dear, I have been giving this a great

deal of thought in the last few seconds and I've concluded that you need a giant dose of sex, liberally applied."

"I have *plenty* of sex," she said, twisting her napkin. "Tons of it. Just not always with you is all."

"I have noticed your absence from my bed, except when we watch TV."

"Which is never," she said.

"Are you hinting I buy one? They have color now, I understand."

She squinted and whispered, "Don't turn now, but there is a man at the next table who's making eyes at me."

I turned. A man in a shiny blue suit and bulging blue eyes. And a grotesque plaid tie. He was still staring. "Maybe he knows you from one of your reading groups."

"Does he look like he's into Proust?"

"Or maybe your spin class?"

"That butterball?"

"Or maybe from your Umbrian cooking class or your Zen poetry workshop? Maybe he's your old college boyfriend gone chubby and bald?"

"He had no friends. He got rich before he could make any."

"Excuse me," I said. "Must see a man about a horse."

"That same old, tired nag? Is he still running?"

"More frequently than ever."

The bathroom was white and empty, palatial in size and bracing in its mountain pine–scented aroma. It was pleasant to be alone in a room without the hum of voices. But suddenly a man materialized at the adjacent urinal, but he was not peeing. His blue suit went dull in the fluorescent light.

"Is that your wife?"

"None other," I replied.

"Because it's unnatural for a husband and wife to talk so much at dinner. Unless they're newlyweds. Are you newlyweds?"

I zippered up and went to wash my hands. The water was warm and flowed luxuriously and, for the moment, made me feel secure in this daunting world.

"She's very beautiful, in a fading kind of way," he said, giving his hands a rinse and a shake over the sink.

"Oh! Yes, I agree, both the beauty and the fading part. She aged years at that place."

"Hospital?" he asked with a little alarm in his voice. I pretended not to hear. Until he repeated, "Hospital?"

"No," I said sotto voce, "*prison.*"

I put my hands under a machine and a sheet of brown paper came out with a whine. Then I did it again.

He held the door open for me. "Serious offense?"

I made a face, as if the memory of that time had made me sad, frightened. "She gouged out her lover's eye with a salad fork."

"My God!" he said. "That beautiful woman? Really?"

He opened the door and motioned for me to pass

first. I did the same for him and we went back and forth until finally I won.

He walked beside me, searching, I thought, for something to say, until we reached the dining room, when he whispered, "Good luck, fella."

"He came right over after you left," she said. "And slid a note under my napkin."

"Saying what?"

"Nothing. Just a phone number with an upstate area code."

"Oh! Not Syracuse or Hornell, I hope," I said. She let it pass.

"Well, I suppose I've still got it," she said with a sigh that I liked.

"It has never left you."

Luis threw up his hands. I looked at my watch. We had only five minutes before the concert and we sped to the elevator, where Blue Suit was standing.

My wife smiled at him. "Haven't we met before?"

"I don't think so," he said.

"Oh! Yes, yes, yes," she sang, "I'm sure we have."

The door opened and we entered, my wife first. The man said, "Go ahead. I just forgot I left something at the table."

The door shut. I pressed the button and took her hand and soon we were speeding down to the museum's lobby and to its theater.

"Which story did you tell him?"

"The fork in the eye," I said.

"That's getting tired," she said.

I agreed. The door glided open, and we walked out hand in hand. "You have a new perfume?"

"Yes, do you like it?"

"Love it. Like rags soaked in a dying man's urine."

"That good?"

"Like a sewer overflow in Fez."

"Don't flatter."

She took my arm and leaned her head on my shoulder. "My man," she purred.

We found our seats and, having found them, sat, me on the aisle, where I could close my eyes and fall asleep in the event the performance went flat, without fire or even a flame. And there vanishes two hours.

"You can sleep on my shoulder, if you like," she said.

This was a comforting invitation. Enough to keep me uncomplaining while we waited for the concert to begin. The audience, with its coughing and rustling, seemed impatient—pissed off with life, even. But they did not have her elegant shoulder to anticipate should life go sour.

"Or 'lie in your lap,' madame?"

"Even there, but no snoring."

Finally, the musicians filed out, sat, fidgeted, tuned up. The man in the blue suit was now in a tux. His bow tie drooped. He wore scuffed street shoes with sloped heels. He looked over the audience and caught my eye.

I smiled. My wife did, too. Then I made a gesture as if gouging out my left eye and smiled again. He turned in an agitated way and said some words to the other three, waiting, poised for him to begin.

"You're going overboard with this," she said.

"Yes," I said, feeling contrite. Then I added, "But he deserves it. What kind of man slips you his phone number behind my back? He didn't have the grace to do it in my presence. And it's not even a Manhattan number."

He gave one more alarmed look our way; then, composing himself, and with a slight nod to the others, he ravaged the strings with his bow. It was an accomplished modernist piece, light on melody, heavy on dissonance. It had its innocuous merits, like most intellectually constructed art—like most conventional exchanges in life.

I soon let the music became wallpaper to my thoughts. Which ran this way: Should we stop for a drink after? Why am I so happy? What is it that moves me in life and in art? To the last, I answered, The surprise. Then I whispered to myself, She is my marvelous surprise.

There was a silence, a pause before the next piece began, a Beethoven string quartet. The first three movements demanded concentration, diligence, and sent my mind straining to follow its ravishing complexity, but the fourth movement unexpectedly sprang a sweet melody seemingly unrelated to anything in the earlier movements and my heart opened with a warm tenderness to life, even if the illness and dying part were to come sooner rather than later.

I barely knew the music was over when the audience rose about me, clapping. My wife released my hand and started clapping wildly. I sat but did not clap; I was in a daze of bliss and could hardly move. We left our seats slowly, lingering, as if to savor the rare thing that had happened to us. And we were the last to take our coats and the last at the long steps leading down to the street, where the waiting taxis fled into the night.

"Cab?" I asked.

"I'd rather hoof it, is what I'd rather do. Wait, didn't we get mugged walking here last year?" she said.

"The kids sort of just asked us for money."

"Was it the knives that opened your wallet?"

"That, and I liked that they called me 'sir.'" We walked. She nestled into my arm.

"You're okay," she said.

"So was the violinist."

"Very okay. Very," she said.

Before we knew it, we were at the Carlyle. "This is a kir royale night," I said.

"Sure, you get one," but then, turning to the bartender, she said, "Monsieur Marcel, I'll have a Seven and Seven and a Corona." He brought us a crystal bowl of nuts, not a peanut among them.

"Do you have any pretzels, Marcel?"

"*Je n'en ai pas,*" he said.

"The next time, I'm going to bring you a few boxes to keep for me, with my name on them."

"*Quelle bonne idée,*" he said.

He brought us our drinks, excused himself, and sped to the other end of the bar, where a young couple in party hats was flagrantly in love.

"We should have died right there in our seats after the final movement. But it would have been inconsiderate of the others in our row, I suppose," she said.

"I guess, and we wouldn't have wanted to spoil his night, even if he's so tacky," I said.

"He's tacky, all right, but brilliant. One doesn't preclude the other."

"Right, just look at Wagner."

"He wasn't at all tacky. Wagner was rotten and sexy." She took a slug of beer straight from the bottle. I had never seen her do that before.

"You've never seen me do that before," she said, reading my mind. "Well, I thought I'd put a little spice in my life. Like that girl over there."

The girl was dividing her time between guzzling her beer and tonguing her boyfriend. I heard Marcel say to the lovers, "I have asked you twice politely to behave. Please leave now. Go to the St. Regis for this kind of material."

"We have a room here," the young man said with nervous dignity.

"Then, should you continue, I shall have you evicted," Marcel said.

Marcel returned to us. "*Incroyable, ça, n'est-ce pas?*"

"*Pas de tout,*" my wife said. "*Les bêtises de jeunesse.*"

"I myself was once young, but even in my youth I observed the proprieties," Marcel said.

Some people came in noisily and settled at the only empty table. It was the musicians with their bulging instrument cases and two young women gleeful to be with them.

Marcel beckoned to the waiter and said, "Tell them they must install their instruments in the cloakroom. We cannot have them cluttering the bar."

My wife gave them a smile and waved hello. I made a friendly nod to the table and a little bow to the first violinist, now again in his blue suit. He smiled back like a man hiding a toothache.

"Marcel, please send them over a bottle of champagne," my wife said. "You choose, you always know the best."

"I shall take care of it," Marcel said. "A good-quality champagne, of course, but nothing too grand."

"Sending only a bottle, my dear?" I asked.

"It's just for the gesture, not to make a drama of the thing," she said.

The table went into a huddle; the violinist leaned in and spoke. A few moments later, they all turned, giving us looks of wonder and discomfort.

"Let's go before the champagne arrives," she said. "I'd feel more comfortable."

"Sure, that will leave a trail of mystery behind." I signed our tab and slid a bill into Marcel's hand.

"*Bonsoir*, Marcel," she said, blowing him a kiss.

"*Bonne soirée, monsieur-dame*," Marcel said, giving the bar counter a swipe of his immaculate towel.

We got to our building as it began to snow. "Oh! Let's stay and watch the snow fall on the trees," she said. "It's been such a rare night. I hate for it to end so quickly."

We paused under the canopy as the snow fell in a greater and greater rush. Eddie, the doorman, stood guard at the doorway and gave us a friendly smile and a salute.

"Have you ever observed that the snow is gentler on this side of the park?"

"I've noticed that, too," she said. "And that the flakes are more distinguished."

Eddie came over and asked if we'd like him to bring out our beach chairs so that we could sit under the canopy.

"We're not staying that long. Unless you want to," she said, taking my hand.

"We're fine, Eddie. Thank you very much," I said, making a note to tip him before we went up. Tips, big ones especially, make the world run on time; I had learned that in Paris, where even love affairs run on time.

We sometimes sat in front of the building on spring

nights to gawk at the stars and at the flow of the Fifth Avenue traffic. We blighted the sidewalk, several of our neighbors protested in anonymous letters. One wrote, "Move to the Bronx." We received official reprimands from the board, until my wife, the litigation lawyer, threatened to sue them. She never seemed to mind the cold shoulders after that. I think she was glad for them. She was silent in the ride up the elevator and was distracted in our apartment, looking out the window several times into the now fiercely driving snow.

"It's coming down hard now," she said. "How will the musicians ever get home tonight?"

"You mean the musician," I said.

"His shoes are too thin for the snow." She looked away for a moment before kissing me on the cheek and saying, "Good night, sweet dreams."

I went to my bedroom, undressed, and put on my comforting blue flannel pajamas with prancing polar bears. I thought about the music I had heard earlier and how Beethoven shaved sounds into planes, each note hiding another that could not be heard but was vibrantly felt. I was still thinking about this when she came in without knocking.

"Would you like a visit?" she asked.

"For as long as you wish," I said.

"It's just a visit," she said; "I wasn't thinking of moving in." She was in oversize boy's pajamas with wild horses roaming a range of hills and sky. She slid under the covers and took the book from my hand.

"Lights on or off?" she asked. Before I could answer, she added, "It's been so long, maybe lights off is better. I don't want to shock you with the changes."

"You never change," I said. "You are one of those immutable forms of nature."

"Sure," she said, switching off the light.

She took off her pajamas. I could see even in the faint window light the scars from her old operations and the recent gash where her breast had been. We kissed, a little formally. It had been so long, I was shy. But soon we kissed like first lovers. We lay still, bathed in the faint glow of the streetlamps and the reflecting light of the snow on the windowsill.

"I don't love you," she said, taking my hand. "I don't love you very much."

"Same here with aces," I said.

We kissed again before she went back to her room. She had left my door open, but I was too comfortable in my place to get up to shut it. Images of her played in my mind until I finally fell into a mellow sleep. It was almost two when I heard my wife's low voice, but she was not in my room. I first thought she was sleep talking, though over the years I had rarely heard her do so. I waited awhile, but I grew worried that she was unwell, so I went to her door, which was open. The light was on and the bed was in disarray. She looked up, her cell phone in her hand.

"I called him to apologize for the bad joke. I called to say how great he was. It was a perfect evening and I did not want it to end with regrets, that's all."

"You called him at three in the morning?"

"Musicians never sleep, don't you know that?"

I stayed silent and troubled. And finally, I said, "I see."

"Look, my dear," she said, "We've had a good life and a night we'll never top. What's the point, then, of our waiting around for all the dreariness to come?"

"Well, there's life is why."

"So you can see me sliced up again? So you can sit in a hospital corridor waiting for the news?"

"There's nothing to worry about yet. Go back to sleep," I said with all the tenderness and assurance I could bring to my voice.

I went back to bed. It was some while before I could return to sleep, but not before I heard her on the phone again. I felt a mild nausea sweep over me and I turned off the light.

It was early morning when she came into the room fully dressed. "I'll be gone for a little while now," she said. "Maybe for the day. Or so."

"Going out in this snow?"

"Don't worry, Eddie will get me a cab."

"Will you stay for breakfast?"

"Just start without me."

"I'll wait," I said. I walked her to the door and watched her put on her sable coat and matching Russian sable hat. She looked as if she were going on a sleigh ride in 1904 to meet her lover in a dacha in Siberia.

After she left, I started puttering about. Walked into the kitchen, then walked out, put on Ravel's *Pavane pour une infante défunte*, but its melancholy only further dispirited me and gloomed up the furniture. I looked for solace and read aloud to myself Wallace Stevens's "Sunday Morning." Did he ever love anything but metaphor and the immutable, imperishable forms of beauty? These and other lofty thoughts did not distract me from the snow and my wife, who was out there in it. Or out there somewhere. I soon found that I was in no mood to read or to do much of anything but brood

I phoned down to the desk and Eddie answered. "Was my wife able to get a cab?" I asked.

"I told her she'd never get one in this snow. She said that was okay, that she didn't want one anyway."

I paced the apartment again, this time looking for our dear cat, Nicolino, knowing he was not there, having died years ago, his little dried-up body found in one of the building's shafts. She cried for a week and said we should never have a cat again. And we didn't. But we had his ghost, who showed up mostly at our breakfast, the meal he had always loved best to share with us in his mortal form.

The snow was piling up on the windowsill and the park faded into whiteness; the trees seemed embarrassed by the weight of their heavy white shapes. I went back to the kitchen. The fridge was almost empty, but there was a little tin of caviar our friends had given us two weeks ago. Our friends, a middle-aged couple like us, had come to celebrate our twentieth anniversary and they were merry all through dinner, but I knew they were unhappy together—their pores leaked it—and were yearning to return home to settle back into the familiar comfort of their unhappiness. I thought not to open the caviar lest it release the unhappiness they had brought with it, and I returned the tin to its cold place. Anyway, I could always one day share it with Nicolino, who wasn't so fussy about human emotions.

Eddie phoned. "The city's shut down," he said, "I had to sleep on the couch in the hall."

"It must be cold down there," I said, "Come up and have a drink."

"No, you come down," he said, "and let's have a snowball fight." He was drunk again.

I got dressed and went to the cabinet and pulled out an unopened bottle of malt scotch that someone had left us years ago and took two glasses from the kitchen, one for Eddie. Why not get drunk together, I thought. Maybe we could even make a snowman at the entrance and irritate the other tenants.

He was sprawled on the hall couch, gaudy with parrots

and monkeys sitting in leafy tropical branches. He fit the scene, even with his winter coat and Russian-style fur hat that my wife had given him after our return from a Siberian vacation. His eyes were open, but the rest of him was asleep. I left the bottle and the glasses—crystal, for the occasion—by the couch and went to the doorway, halfway blocked by the snow. I pushed my way out and into the pathway now covered with crunchy snow high to my knees. I took the shovel that Eddie had left by the door and cut a path to the sidewalk. A bus had careened into a tree and stood, lights on, with snow embracing the tires. No cars passed, nor did one person in the tundra of lampposts of what once had been Fifth Avenue. The passengers and driver, I surmised, had made their way out earlier, because their tracks were now covered in the snow, as I now was fast becoming.

I felt a terrible chill once I was back in the building that not even a stiff drink of the scotch that I had brought down with me seemed to warm. The bottle had been opened and I could see from the half-filled glass on the floor that the now fully awake Eddie had not stood on ceremony.

"Excellent scotch," Eddie said, raising his glass in a toast. "To you and the missus."

"To you and yours, Eddie," I said, feeling the warmth returning, feeling a bit of good cheer even.

"There is no mine, Mr. Charles." And then, rising from his prone position and sitting erect but wobbling slightly, he added, "There is no nothing. That's the ticket, no nothing. One day she's holding my hand in the park on a bench under a big fat tree with leaves so green that your eyes water and calling me 'sweetie' and 'honey' and 'cupcake' and me returning the same to her with interest and the next day she's in a hospital with arms stuck with needles and before you can say 'jackrabbit,' she's ashes in a jar."

"I'm so sorry, Eddie," I said. I was sorry. For him, for us. For all of us. Where was she now, in all this whiteout?

"Stick with your missus as long as you can. Even if you can't stand it once in a while."

"Keen advice, Eddie."

He sloshed his glass with a hefty dose of scotch and knocked it back. It seemed to sober and steady him and he straightened himself and stood up erect like a marine at drill. "*Le silence d'amour. Ce n'est tout, ne c'est pas?*"

"*Bien sûr,*" I said, a bit astonished that Eddie spoke French and with a Parisian flair, *en plus.* One day I would introduce him to Marcel and hear them discourse on the proprieties of love.

Thinking of love, I asked, "By the way, have you seen Nicolino these days?"

"He passes by to say hello sometimes and vanishes into the park."

I was very sad that he had not come to see me in months, and my expression showed it.

"He's got a girlfriend. He's in love, I can tell."

"In love," I said.

"Yes, Mr. Charles, but I'm sure he will never leave you. *Jamais.*"

I left Eddie and the half-empty scotch bottle with him. And without further word, he stretched out on the couch and went back to sleep in the jungle drunk with acrobatic apes and screaming parrots.

No sooner had I settled in and returned to my fears and gloom than the doorbell chimed. Odd that, because Eddie had not phoned to announce a visitor—unless he was so plastered that an elephant could walk by him unnoticed—and I was taken aback. I thought it might be my neighbor, but he and wife had gone to Marrakesh, where they spent their winters in their rented villa packed with their English guests from Belgravia.

But then there was a not too gentle knock and a voice: "I'm frozen. Open up."

She was drowned in snow, so, too, her shopping bags, like baby igloos. She took off her snow-piled coat and hat, dropped them on the marble hall floor, and brought the igloos into the kitchen, brushing off the snow in the wide sink.

"Look what I have," she said, naming each item as she placed it on the kitchen counter: "Lox, sable, salmon roe, bagels, pickles, herring, potato salad, Spanish olives stuffed with almonds, chopped liver, a container of young pickles, Carr's water biscuits, *The New York Times*—it's yesterday's—and Dr. Brown's Cel-Ray soda."

"Wasn't everything closed?"

"Everything is. The whole city is closed. The owner at the deli was trapped there overnight and he welcomed me like a rescue party. Half the stuff here is a present."

"Eddie's been down there all night. Let's invite him up for breakfast—or bring him down a tray."

"Later, if you like. I just want breakfast alone with you, unless you've got some floozy stashed away here."

"Please, her name's Brandee. She's a model slash astrophysicist, and she left a minute ago."

"Okay," she said, "then let's get down to business."

She loaded up a tray with the deli containers and I took out the plates and silverware and we set up on the dining room table. She disappeared for what seemed forever but returned with a silver pot of coffee and a creamer. I noticed that she had changed into a Chinese silk robe where dragons clashed and fire streamed from their eyes.

"Have you missed me?"

"Not at all," I said.

"So robust of you!"

"Missed you the whole world," I added.

She poured coffee into my cup and pitched in a bit of cream—the way she knew I liked it.

"Have you ever wanted to be invited to a party just for the satisfaction of not going?" she asked. "Have you?"

"I'm no longer invited to parties," I said, "nor do I wish to be."

"Then what would you know, Louis, of the pleasure of not showing up?"

I wanted to kiss her but thought better of it, not to change the mood. We didn't speak for a long while, eating lazily, as if we had all the time in the world.

L'Odyssée

Then I made me way into the house itself and found it all in shambles. A clothesline freighted with underwear, not mine, and three pairs of long johns, not mine, stretched across the living room. The bathroom reeked of men's aftershave and colognes—Brut—and all was littered with gum stimulators, nose-hair scissors, mustache trimmers, nail cutters, and other implements and toiletries that I never use.

The bedroom. The bedroom. It stabbed me heart. Men's boots and shoes of various sizes and shapes, quality and age were lined along the wall. But not one pair of mine in the lot.

"What! That you?" she said, pulling down the edge of her slinky black negligee.

I was charged with great emotion, seeing her spread out there in our old bed, seeing her changed not a jot in all the years I had been gone. Not one wrinkle, not one gray hair, not one bump or wart or blemish. She was her old skinny self with a few new appealing curves, her tongue still as sharp as her pointy elbows.

Before I could answer her, Nestor, with all the juice of his youth dried out of him, limped into the room—where was his fourth leg?—and gave me a steady look and a short sniff. Sniff sniff, like a sneeze that had fallen asleep; then he turned about and limped out the door as if I were not there, had never lived there, would never again live there.

"Nestor," I cried, "it's me."

Not a glance me way. He may be deaf, I thought, seeing him slouch off like an old man with a missing leg, *en plus.* Age and loss. Twin themes I had thought would never visit me.

"Yes, it's me come home," I said as she rose from the bed and wrapped about her a great green housecoat, which covered her from foot to neck—her head sticking out like a white bean squeezed from its pod.

"Returned home like the faithful sailor you are. Away for a thousand years and never a postcard."

"It's a long and odd story, me dear, and one I'm eager to tell."

"The world may be all ears, but I'm not," she said. "Your berth's been taken, sailor, so cast off."

She was her same wonderful biting self but with a decidedly new and attractive twist. Her once long and sharp toenails were now trim and shaded rose. Her feet, peeking out from under her robe, usually rough and dry like barnacles, were presently smooth and, dare I say, creamy. Dare I say fetching!

She glowed in her new *soigné* self. Or is it *soignée* self?—I have never mastered the niceties of French grammar. In short, she looked swell. I had a strong, sudden rise of feeling for her, which caught her eye.

"That broken mast of yours? That midget sea worm? That slack line, here again?" Her chuckle froze the furnace in me heart.

She brushed by me in a breeze of jasmine and swept into the kitchen, where I followed in her wake. She poured herself a mug of java, black and without refinements.

"And me?" I asked, wishing so much for a cup of true American coffee, spiced with sugar and cream. And maybe some slices of Wonder bread or a kaiser roll with a few pats of butter and jam on the side. It had been so long.

"There's the diner across the way," she said, pointing with a hand loaded with glittering rings. I sank under this humiliation, me, the descendent of Hercules and the sometimes master of me fate. I looked about me to conceal the sad unfairness of me welcome. The open shelves were bursting with canned goods, mostly pickled meats and exotic soups, but not one tin of spinach. And above me hung hams and sausages of all nations, garlands of garlic and fierce red peppers, and cheeses, too, hanging in the morning breeze and sun of the open window. I could smell the sea outside and hear its salty churn mixing with the rumble of voices and their medley of languages.

"I suppose," I said at last, "I'll grab me tackle and be on me way."

She softened at seeing me unhappy and in a kindly voice said, "Pour yourself a cup, then, but don't be all day about it."

I sat in a block of stone, granite I think, unable to move, until she said, "Look here, I'll do it for you, as you seem out of sorts."

"Forgive me," I said, "I have not been in a house or at a table or with a spoon to stir me cup for many years, and I came to believe that I never would again."

"Oh!"

"And I did not think that I would ever again see your face, although that was all I ever did wish."

"I did not recognize you at first," she said, "with your rough beard and white hair, with your sunken cheeks and starved eyes."

"It's me all the same," I said, brightening a little at the friendly tone in her voice.

Then she laughed and added, "Well then, if it really be you, say it for me."

At first, I did not know what she had meant, and I cudgeled me brain and all its rafters to bring it to proper recollection.

At last, it hit me: "*Je suis ce que je suis,*" I said.

"You're a fake, a fraud, trying to trick me like all the others out there!"

"*Non, non,*" I protested, "*un imposteur, moi! Ce n'est pas vrai.*"

She went for a broom and made to sweep me away like some old dust underfoot. "Clear out," she said; "scuttle along, you devious slug!"

But then, in a bolt of memory, I finally got me native language back and I said, "I yam what I yam."

"There you are!" she said, pouring me another cup of java. But then, fearful, it seemed, she had gone too far in warming to me, she added, "And there you go, because nothing's changed that you went away without a word and stayed away with a word."

"Not me fault," I said. But before I could continue, she said with a kind of xenophobic fury, "And what's with the Frenchy stuff anyways?"

I saw no point in more palaver. I did what any manly American man would do and went into action instead of talking more talk. I rose up and took the broom from her hand and planted one on her lips, a kiss to make up for all the lost years, a kiss to send stars spinning over her head. When we at last unlocked, she said in a voice throaty and sexy, "Take off your cap and let me have a good lookatya."

I did so and flattened down me hair and licked me upper teeth for a brushing. She gave me another long look and said, "I know what's missing, my dearie." She went into a cabinet and drew out, hidden behind boxes of cereal, one of me old pipes, which she plugged with tobacco and lit with a match the length of an arrow.

"This is better than any dream I ever had when I was in me cage and dreaming of returning home."

"Your cage?" she said, alarmed for the past me.

"Yes, me dear, me iron cage," I said. Then I went right down to it and told her how I had been drugged and shanghaied one night and sold to be the strongman in a traveling circus, *l'Odyssée* the troupe *s'appellait,* for it was French straight down to every nail and peg.

"Oh! Dear!" she said, her eyes widening into saucers.

"By day, I was fed food laced with flowery drugs that kept me lazy and sleepy and content to stay in me cage, and at night, just before showtime, they spooned me just the right amount of spinach to give me the strength to rassle lions and bears and gorillas, to do tugs-of-war with elephants, and to break giant cables wrapped about me chest. The drugs kept me in a haze of forgetfulness of all I had ever lived or been, but sometimes your memory and our life together with our son would penetrate the haze and I would scheme to escape."

"Oh, Popeye!"

"But I was guarded day and night by a one-eyed man who slept on a cot by the side of the cage—he was the fire-eater, one of the show's main attractions and a partner in the circus, so he had every reason to keep me a prisoner—a slave—as I was a big money draw."

"But weren't you recognized by the audience?" she asked suspiciously. "The world knows you!"

"Not with the mask they kept over me head when I performed—a papier-mâché mask of me own head."

"How clever!" she said. "A mask of you to mask you!"

"And," I continued, "everyone from the grub man to the ringmaster spoke only French, and after a few years I lost me own language and I spoke only French, but a debased form of it, which was mocked by all but the show animals, who, I should say, came to love me as I did them, we being of the same captive stuff. Even the singing eagle and the chorus of her ferocious brood loved me. So, too, the elephant family I taught how to play poker—jokers wild—and the dancing python, too, all friends under the same tent."

I was going on with me story, when I heard the voices out the window grow louder and more belligerent. She looked at me as if to say, "See what you have come home to?"

"Who is out there," I asked, "in our courtyard?"

"The ones waiting for you never to come back, the ones waiting for me to fall into their laps." So, it was true. I had been forewarned of all this by the fortune-teller at the circus. I would find me wife's suitors and claimants at me home, rioting at me door when at last I returned home, she had said, reading tea leaves drowning in a cup. I went out to the courtyard to see what was what. Fifty men were milling about, from ages twenty-five to sixty-eight, some bleary-eyed and disheveled from having slept in a chair or in a sleeping bag, and some spanking fresh and ready to take on the world, each man the rival of the others and all the rival of me.

"Pipe down," I said. "You're disturbing the peace."

"Beat it, pops," a lad with a biker's helmet said, twirling a chain.

"Go home, grandpa," shouted another, who was wearing a tailored suit and creamy pink tie. I could see a pistol bulging under his jacket.

I realized then how old and worn-out and weak I looked, like a beggar who has been wandering for years along dusty back roads. I realized, too, that with all the changes to meself, I had gone unrecognized and was nothing but bones with a beard that had come to beg for shelter. I heard a piercing cry high above me and saw an eagle, me old friend from the circus, circling there in long, strong loops, and it gave me a good cheer.

I said nothing to their jeers and returned to the kitchen to continue me story. To finish with that piece of business before going to another.

"Be patient," I said. "We'll get to the heart and matter of these people outside in a little while."

She looked at me with a friendly pity, as if to say, "I know you would do the best you could in ridding us of this trash, but look at you; you seem too weak even to climb a ladder." I took her arm, touching her for the first time since I had come home. So soft her skinny arm, so beautiful. The noise out in the courtyard grew even louder than when I had gone out there, and this time there were shouts and calls for fistfights and battles with knives and baseball bats.

"Perhaps we should just disappear," she said, "steal away and leave them to themselves while we sail elsewhere and chart a new course."

"And give up the house and the garden and the wide veranda that fronts and hangs over the sea, give up me chumming rights and me clam beds and lobster traps, give up me dinghy with its one green mast, give up me son, whom I have yet to see in his grown years, give up me bed that I built with me own hands from the planks and beams of noble three-masters driven to the rocks in shattering tempests, the bed I anchored down to the living granite beneath me house, give up you, in whose eyes I will have become a mollusk without courage or a spine?"

I could see her brood on this a while, little ringlets of smoke curling about her ears as they did when she was given to serious thought or was about to grow angry.

"I see your point," she said, folding her arms into several knots.

"Bear with me awhile," I said, "because I have not come home without contrivances or hope." I was about to return to me tale of how I had escaped the circus, how I had tricked the one-eyed guard to open me cage, and how I had blinded him with one quick plunge of me pipe stem and stolen the keys to all the cages while he had writhed about in the cold straw of me cell. To tell how I had set free all me animal friends, including a giant tortoise whose shell glowed in the dark and sent weather signals to the mermaids at sea. But then I heard great roars of laughter and derision, and I poked me head out the window to see me old friend Wimpy in his great brown tweed suit being dangled by his ankles over the veranda rail. His bowler was waiting for him, floating in the ocean below.

One of the men dangling him, a giant with bowling pins for arms, spied me and called out, "Come out here, old man, and get some of the same."

That did it. I could stands no more. I went to the bathroom and scissored off the greater part of me wild beard and lathered up what stubble was left on me face and shaved it down to the smoothest old man's baby skin. Then I took off me shirt and sprinkled some water over me chest and stringy neck. The tattoo on me forearm was fading into the bowels of me skin, but there was enough of the blue anchor showing to tell the world just who it was playing with. I gave me teeth a proper brushing until those pearls looked newborn from their shell. In all, I didn't look a day older than fifty.

"Oh! Here's my man," she said on my return to the kitchen. "Here's the one I waited for and would gladly wait for again."

"Yes, Olive, me dearie. I'm home at last."

She rummaged behind a shelf of beef and soup cans,

her arm sinking deep into its depths, until she drew out a musty old tin.

"I've saved this for you," she said, opening the can. "Do you want it on a plate or will you take it straight?"

I downed the spinach in two swallows. And could feel me strength returning to me in a warm current.

"Now, be my champion!" she said.

I planted another one on her, smack on the lips, until little moons spun about our heads. I stepped onto the veranda and looked up to the sky and signaled the spiraling eagle, who sent out a cry summoning all the circus animals who were waiting nearby to help me retake me home. The tortoise lumbered along, sending signals to the mermaids to swim to our aid. The elephants blew their great trumpets, calling the waves to fearful heights; the lions breathed mighty roars that split clouds; the python hissed with a cold slicing sound that melted rocks; the gorillas beat their chests and cursed in gutter French. I watched as me allies gathered force, and then I sallied forth with me naked arm to set the world to right.

CODA

Some Episodes in the History of My Reading

The Bed

My mother comes home from work tired. We sit in the kitchen with my grandmother, who has prepared a frugal meal, and by nine my mother is off to bed. We do not have a TV—it is 1945, and few do in my Bronx neighborhood—so I read a library book, a Jules Verne, maybe, or an abridged version of *The Three Musketeers.* The living room, with my wheezing grandmother sleeping fitfully behind the screen that separates us, my squeaky cot and the old, thin blankets, the winter coldness, all suddenly vanish. I'm ten and carried into the richest worlds of life and remain there as long as I'm reading my book. And I'm protected from harm after I turn off the light as long as the book remains in my hand.

The Raft

My mother gave me *The Adventures of Tom Sawyer* and *The Adventures of Huckleberry Finn* for my eleventh birthday. She had heard that they were what American boys read. I devoured the Twain books over and over again, finding myself in them—that is, my desired, adventurous, free self. Finding in Tom and Huck the friends I needed and wanted, models to keep me in the hope of escape from my cramped world in the Bronx. I was raised by Sicilians and I may as well have been living in Palermo, where there was no vast Mississippi and no wide raft to ride it, no open sky and no territory ahead, no America.

I lived not far from the mighty ripple of the Bronx River, and one afternoon I tied a small raft of planks I had plucked from a construction site close to the Botanical Garden—where the river ran through—then still on the wild side, with a deer or two hiding in the brush. I left my shoes and socks on the bank and pushed off and sank. I got stuck in the river's soft, muddy bottom and barely worked my way out of the muck. I was coated in watery mud and crying with fear on the grassy bank. I wonder what story I told my mother when she saw me mud-caked and trembling. That was the early end of my exotic adventures. I consigned them to the safer regions of movies and books and, later, to putting them into my own fiction, in novels and stories located far from the Mississippi, far from America, and about artists, revolutionaries, and romantics, who, unlike me, burn and dare.

The Seduction

When I was young, I sought the more difficult books, the more difficult the better: I did not ever want to be led to where and what I had already known, to be guided in a language with words that seldom required a dictionary. At fifteen, I saw Caroline, an older woman, on whom I had a giant crush, sitting on a park bench and reading as if nothing else in the world mattered. I was ashamed of my lustful thoughts and expected her to have read them in my stare. She finally noticed me and called me over and asked if I liked to read.

"Of course," I said, and nervously began to name a few books I loved.

"Those are good books. You're my son's friend, aren't you?"

"Yes, I am," I said, not mentioning that we disliked each other, that he called me four eyes and a fruity bookworm.

"I have other books you may like," she said, "so come by for coffee." Her apartment jumped with books, shelves of them even in the kitchen, where we sat and drank coffee and where I burned for her. She lent me the novel she had been reading on the park bench, Djuna Barnes's *Nightwood*. "Let me know what you think," she said. I wanted to like it because she had. I wanted to like it because I wanted her to like me. But I couldn't follow the story; I did not understand if there was a story, but there were passages of intense, mysterious beauty that made me tremble as I had on my first Holy Communion.

(That early reaction apart, I came, as I grew older, to understand how daring and rebellious *Nightwood* is. Barnes sidesteps the rules of normative—and predictable—fiction. The rules so beloved and enforced by the writing professors. Barnes tells and does not always show; she comments on her characters, even excoriating one; she shuns writing dialogue that supposedly replicates the way people speak—or are thought to speak; she abandons the so-called requisite arc of the narrative and for two chapters plunges into some of the most forceful prose poetry written on the mystery of love and whom we love. For her independence in life and in her art, she is my model.)

A year later, I broke my head trying to make sense of Joyce's *Ulysses*, another book Caroline gave me, one she had a special passion for. Something extraordinary was going on there in that Irishman's ocean of words, and I felt elevated, special, just trying to fathom it. But what remained in me was not only the novels she had led me to but the association of fiction with sexual longing, and with beauty and mystery.

Caroline loved *Ulysses* so much that she left her husband and children to live in Paris with a French scholar who had devoted his life to that one book. His passion for what she also loved was the magnet. Because of her, I'm drawn to any woman I see reading a book and curious to know what she is reading, snobbishly gauging her desirability by her taste.

Once, at Café de Flore in Paris, I saw an elegant woman, as Henry James would say, of a certain age, fixed on a book. She was at the same table over the following five days. Once, our eyes met and we smiled. I took the courage from that smile to approach her and ask in my most polite way, and in my halting French, what she was reading.

"*Nightwood*," she said, showing me the cover. "And you?"

I held back my surprise and my wanting to tell her how I had first come across the book, but instead I replied, "*The Third Policeman*, by an Irish writer. I'm not sure it's translated."

"I have read it in English," she said, adding, "I have wondered what you were reading all these days and wondered if you were a simpleton."

She did not appear the next day or the days after, which I ascribed to my barging in on her privacy. But the headwaiter, Marcel, a man I had known for years and who was a friend of the novelist Lawrence Durrell, said, "She comes here every spring and early fall for seven days and sits with a book, speaks to no one, and waits for no one. She is not French and she is not English or American.

She drinks calvados in Coca-Cola and smokes cigarettes in a holder. She leaves extravagant tips above the *service compris,* so we don't care how long she sits, even when we are busy. We admire her comportment." I imagined her in a world of books and art and intellectual elegance and wrote a novel about her called *The Green Hour.*

The Poisonous Book

A novel may just leave you where you were when you started it, and in that case, it was not worth your time, the dear hours of your life never returned. Sometimes, and in the best case, a novel leaves you with a shudder of recognition—about what you do not know: It has altered you and you do not understand how or why, but it has. That does not mean it has changed you to be kinder or not to cheat on your lover or on your income taxes. But it has changed you: However alone, you are not completely alone.

W. H. Auden said that poetry changes nothing but the nature of its saying. That may be true for poetry, but fiction's power moves in mysterious ways. Some novels may elevate you; some may degrade. At eighteen, I encountered a "poisonous book," like the novel given to Dorian Gray by the worldly, corrupt Lord Henry. That novel that turned Dorian into an aesthete who believed there were no rules to limit or govern his wish and pursuit of pleasure. I was in my freshman year at City College and doing poorly—because I arrogantly, rebelliously read everything but the required texts. The final exams would determine if I was going to be expelled, which, for me, meant the street. I started to study four days before the exams. I liked the danger of it, the immersion of life at the brink's edge. Of course, I slept little and drank black coffee and smoked until my eyes popped; that was part of the ritual, but one that deranged me. The week before the exam, I had lit on *The Fountainhead,* sitting on a pile I had taken from the library. I had been warned against it by my fellow bohemian students: It was a fascist book, an apologia for social Darwinism, an all-around rotten business, with cardboard characters to boot.

It didn't matter. I started reading it in the afternoon and through the night and morning of my first exam. I slept for two hours and went off to the subway and down to the college, took the exams, and failed both algebra and biology. I had a semester of academic suspension to mull over my megalomania- and fantasy-driven crimes.

What had happened? Midway in my reading of *The Fountainhead,* the idea grew that I was above exams and above study, towering above the college and above every demand made on me other than my own. And soon I was sure that I would not only pass the exams but that by my powers of concentration I would do brilliantly and win great praise. I was in the clouds of the grand Self. I was like the genius architect, Howard Roark, the superman of Ayn Rand's novel, one of the exceptions for whom rules were meant to be ignored or, better, to be shattered. My fellow students and my professors were the gears that made the System work, that giant academic factory that turned out standard bolts, screws, and solid citizens. I had a higher mission: I was an artist. I was he, Howard Roark of the Bronx. I consoled myself with that idea for a few months after my suspension and while I was distributing mail from desk to desk in a large downtown catalogue company.

Another Book, Another Folly

I suppose I descend from the line of those characters deluded by literature. Don Quixote rides off to save chivalry and the world, modeling himself on an antiquated literature of knights and their codes and adventures; the married Emma Bovary ruins her life in the pursuit of the kind of love she swoons over in the sentimental romances of her day.

My model for ruin was Hemingway. Nothing he could do was wrong. Not a sentence was off. His style was contagious, and many in my generation caught the infection. I wrote shopping lists that read like his: "Buy a true bread. Be sure the *leche* is cold and its container true." His stories were perfect. His life was perfect. Everything Hemingway wrote and did I wanted to write and do. But not exactly: I did not want to fish or hunt. At eighteen, I went out on a day boat that sailed from Sheepshead Bay and moored some miles into the ocean. Within an hour, I turned green and spent the excursion turning even greener belowdecks and pretending to show to the ship's crew—as Hemingway would have me—grace under pressure. As for hunting, at nine, I shot my Red Ryder BB gun at a squirrel squatting in my uncle Umberto's little Bronx garden and missed. I hit my uncle. My uncle was not hurt, but the shot unsettled him, wounded his trust in me. I never again wanted to shoot at any living or inanimate thing.

At nineteen, I went to the corrida in Mexico City because of Hemingway's *Death in the Afternoon*; he had written about the drama of the running of the bulls, and I was sure I would find, as he had, metaphysical courage acted out in the sand. But when the matador's sword plunged in and the bull fell and shuddered and died, I felt ill. I was still sure, however, that the feeling would pass because I would come to see the truth and beauty in the bull's death and in the matador's union with the animal he had just killed. Back in my little hotel, I saw only the felled bull in the blood-soaked sand and I had to drink a lot of tequila before I could finally go to sleep.

From among all of Hemingway's stories, I was especially called to action by "A Clean, Well-Lighted Place," moved by its cadences and glamorous darkness. I liked the idea of a café/bar as a place of sanctuary and that to drink there was a mode of communion with the nothing, the *nada* of the story and of life.

I had learned from Hemingway that it is the writer's

duty to drink. This was much easier than fishing or hunting or even sitting alone and, in total focus and purity of spirit, writing. Hemingway was not all to blame for this, but he had given me a noble mission, an obligation to the profession, which I, as an earnest young man, was eager to fulfill.

I was fresh from meeting Hemingway—crashing his home outside Havana—in early September of 1958. He talked about writing and its need for discipline, but he never mentioned the drinking part of the craft, which I assumed was part of the unspoken code that needed no mentioning.

That fall, as one of my experiments with the writer's life and duties, I went to an Irish bar, one of the few then remaining in Harlem, on my way to a morning class at City College. A long, dark bar, a bowl of hard-boiled eggs, no TV, no radio, no music, just as Hemingway would have wanted it. Just me and the purity of the bar and the bartender dozing by the window to the street, and the early morning still fresh with hope. I looked at myself in the mirror and, quoting from Hemingway's story, said sotto voce, "'Certainly you do not want music. Nor can you stand before the bar with dignity although that is all that is provided for these hours.'" At nine, I ordered a double shot of rye with a beer chaser. Then another.

I left for class feeling pleasantly woozy and glowing with dignity, but then, halfway there, I turned back for another round at the bar to secure the dignity. I missed my classes that day, and the days following, when I renewed the experiments, but they, too, failed, like the raft that had sunk in the Bronx River.

It took me many years beyond my adolescence and adulthood to write my shopping list straight and to cease those and other such adventures in drinking .

A New Love

Years ago, a noted writer asked, "Who over the age of forty still reads novels?" I did, and always with the hope of finding the innocent joy and impress of my early reading. For a while, I took a vacation from fiction and turned mostly to biographies and memoirs and letters, to books on history and art. But enriching as they were, none had power over me or lived as deeply in my imagination.

A few years ago, I found for almost nothing all four volumes of André Gide's *Journals* at a library book sale. I had wanted them forever, for the physical beauty of the books alone and because of their echo from my youth, when Gide was a demigod of literature and whose novel, radical for its time, *The Counterfeiters* I had loved. Gide's reading was wide and profound, and I came to value and trust his taste, a trust that grew volume by volume, and I wanted to read the books he so much cared about. I admired and felt kinship with him because he was not afraid to dislike what the world claims it reveres. He demolishes, for example, *King Lear*: "The entire play from one end to another is absurd" (*The Journals of André Gide*, volume 4). It was reassuring to know that someone else on this planet felt as I had. His praise for Steinbeck's masterpiece strike novel, *In Dubious Battle*, made me value his judgment even more.

So it surprised me to find this 1944 entry: "have just devoured one after another eight books by Simenon at the rate of one a day." And then in 1948, the line "New plunge into Simenon; I have just read six in a row." I had always thought of Simenon as a lightweight crime writer, but once I began reading his books, it was curtains for me. I thought, This is why I still read, because without novels like this, life is just breathing.

Sometimes after a serious Simenon binge, I feel sated, saturated, sick of myself, even, for being so addicted. My reward, as with drugs, is to receive less and less pleasure. I have been chasing the original high to no success, but like a true addict, I always relapse. I ask for little—a great opening, a dazzling seventy-five pages. I expect the letdown. But there is always another of his books to find the high.

Simenon wrote many novels, finishing them sometimes as quickly as in two or three weeks. You can feel the moment when he just had had enough. He speeds through the last third to get over with it and move on to write yet another. Classic seduction: charm, conquer, and flee. He jilts you, but it's worth the ride and the disappointment. Better the inconstant but exciting lover than a faithful but predictable one.

No writer—not even Hemingway—opens his books with such economy and unadorned ease as Simenon does. No one draws you in as quickly on the first paragraph and holds you. No one creates or reveals a character in a phrase or line like he does. In a 1955 *Paris Review* interview, Simenon said that "an apple by Cézanne has weight. And it has juice, everything. With just three strokes. I tried to give to my words just the weight that a stroke of Cézanne's gave to an apple."

In the novel *Madame Maigret's Own Case*, we see a woman turn down to the lowest flame a pot of stew she is cooking. She puts on her coat and hat and, before leaving, quickly checks herself in the mirror and "seeing that everything is all right, rushes out." That little moment illuminates her pride, her vanity, her bourgeois correctness. Simenon makes no mention of her age, height, weight, no description of her hat, coat, shoes, her nose, her hair—all the ponderous, belabored detail that we are told is supposed to make a character vivid, real, and that we immediately forget. But in just a phrase, three strokes, voilà, Simenon's character has volume and personality.

What Simenon does so simply and brilliantly for character he also does in his creation of atmosphere or the mood of his novels. In that same *Paris Review* interview, he said that his sense of atmosphere came from looking at Impressionist paintings when he was a young boy. I can't imagine how he transposed the sunny dispositions of those paintings into the musty hallways and the half-lit, creaking, dingy tenements, the smells of cooking wafting through a window in summer, the yellowish fog over the Seine in the wet fall, the evocation of Paris at a time before Malraux had the grand buildings cleaned and their venerable patina washed down to the gutters and sewers. Simenon's Paris lives before the tearing down of the ancient market at Les Halles, with its vans packed with produce and the little bistros serving onion soup at four in the morning. It almost makes you forget that Simenon is from Belgium or that Paris has changed. His atmospherics envelop his novels but never impede the velocity of the narrative. Velocity is the key.

When asked about Proust, Isaac Singer said, "Does he make you want to turn the page?" Of course Proust does, but to turn it slowly. I'm not suggesting that velocity is the foremost quality that matters in a novel, but the velocity of Simenon's prose sweeps away all the dross, clutter, and manicured verisimilitude of much contemporary fiction. And Simenon pushes aside the idea of writing only "likable" and "relatable" protagonists, the expected staples of standard-issue fiction.

Dirty Snow (published in English in 1951) is set in a small, grisly town in an indeterminate place and time—but clearly during the Nazi occupation of France and Belgium. The master image is of blackened snow, stinking alleyways, dens of steam, smoke, drink, and menace, where a teenager, Frankie, spends his nights. His mother keeps a brothel of two or three girls in her small apartment, where he sleeps and sometimes shares his bed with them. The boy commits murder and robbery for no apparent reason, and tricks a young woman who loves him into sleeping with an older, slimy man. There are murderers in fiction whom one can feel for, who indicate they are a recognizable part of the human tribe—Camus's Meursault, Dostoevsky's Raskolnikov—but Frankie is not one of them. There is nothing redeemable about him, not a shred of decency or feeling or devilish charm that even the most tender-hearted social worker could detect with a microscope.

In *Dirty Snow*, there is no lovable Maigret, Simenon's famous detective, no welcoming cafés and domestic comforts, no Paris of quaint streets and interesting criminals. This town of dirty snow and gray cold is not even a hell crowded with tortured sinners. Here there is crime for which there is punishment, but there is no justice. Simenon's town lives outside of sin, of good and bad, and, like most life, has no boundaries but power. This is the grimmest novel I have ever read. And perhaps the most moral in its truth.

❖

All my life I wanted to be near books, to have them close to me, by me when I eat, beside me in bed, and on the little shelf I built next to the toilet—a trick I learned from Henry Miller's *The Books in My Life.* As a boy, I hated parting with books from the library and was always fined for late returns. In my teens, I haunted the now vanished Book Row on Fourth Avenue in Manhattan and could find the most important, beautiful books in the world for pennies. I did not need fancy bindings and hand-tooled covers; in any case, they do not enrich the literature they harbor. I would carry my newfound treasures in a brown paper shopping bag on the subway, all the way to the upper Bronx, and imagine them piled up alongside my cot and in an already packed unpainted pine and brick bookcase. I read on the subway, on the bus, on lunch and coffee breaks from work after I dropped out of high school. I read when I got home and when my mother went to bed with one of her romances, usually a novel of pirates and the women they seized as booty and for ransom but whom they ended up loving instead. I read three or four books at a time, going from one to another like a hungry man in a hurry. I wanted to have friends but had few, and none had a passion for reading. I wanted to have a girlfriend and go steady, as that was the height of sophistication for teenagers in the early fifties. I had a girlfriend, but she was always busy. Busy with others.

No one was as sure, as steady, as magical, as mysterious, as sexy, as comforting, as life-giving as anything or anyone I found in the novels I took home. All my life there were disasters in the street, sadness on the subway, heartbreak and betrayals in and out of bed; the world was a disaster, but once I walked into my apartment and saw about me my books on their shelves, I was, I am, safe and maybe even brave.

Among my books I still have some I bought or that were given to me when I was fifteen or sixteen. On those, I made a little drawing of my profile on the flyleaf, and wrote the date of purchase and in careful print the words "Pelham Parkway, the Bronx." One was *The Magic Mountain*; another, Bowles's *The Sheltering Sky.* These and the others from the past I took wherever I moved or stored them for my return. As long as they were with me, I had a history, one more vivid and palpable than a photograph could give me. The books brought with them the damp smells of my Bronx apartment and the spring breezes in the Botanical Garden, where I had read them, the cigarette burns where the ashes fell, the coffee stains on the pages where they were read on the kitchen table, the echoes of the operas broadcast on radio WQXR directly from the Metropolitan every Saturday afternoon. I took *The Sheltering Sky* for Bowles to sign when we were teaching together in Tangier in 1981. The book had traveled a long way from the fifties. Bowles asked, "Did someone pound this with a baseball bat?"

Suppose there is an afterlife and there are no books there, just waves of words with nothing to hold, no pages to turn, no aroma of paper and ink and dust.

Even though there is an eternity of time to read, it would not be the same without the physical entity, the book and its earthly cycle from birth to decay, the once sunny, expectant pages moldering into dust along with the owner. I thought of the history of the burials of the great and the ordinary, and the goods taken by the dead for their future life, whole households of pots and pans and furniture for some, spears and axes for others. I want my books with me, the treasures I have loved and amassed along the way.

No simple coffin will do. I need a mausoleum, like that of the robber baron Jay Gould's mansion-size white pile facing Melville's headstone, up in Woodlawn Cemetery, the last subway stop in the Bronx. Mine would have floor-to-ceiling bookcases, carpeted floors, three or four comfortable leather club chairs, and reading lamps with rose silk shades beside them, and a skylight high above my marble sarcophagus. This is a library that I do not and never shall have in life but that I enjoy imagining will be built after my death. Open to the public—for free, of course—twenty-four hours a day, until the end of eternity.

Story Dedications

Winter, 1965 | *For Tom McCarthy*

The Veranda | *For Jill Bialosky*

The Snow on Tompkins Square Park | *For David Salle*

The Bar at Twilight | *For Henry Threadgill*

The Tower | *For Edmund White*

In the Borghese Gardens | *For Gloria De Petriums Colliani Loomis, on her birthday: May 12, 2003*

The Café, the Sea, Deauville, 1966 | *For Daniele Thompson*

Lives of the Artists | *Homage to Joaquín Torres-García*

Allegory: A Parable | *For Hans Ulrich Obrist*

The Phantom Tower | *For Diane Keaton*

Delacroix in Love | *For Steve Martin*

Nine Flowers | *For the artist Ross Bleckner*

The Garden Party | *For the artist Martin Mull*

The Restaurant. The Concert. The Bar. The Bed. *Le Petit Déjeuner.* | *For Karen Marta*

L'Odyssée | *For the artist Jeff Koons*

Some Episodes in the History of My Reading | *For Jenny Diski*

Acknowledgments

I want to thank the following people for their part in this book:

Karen Marta, for her scrupulous reading, for her constancy, patience, and unabated encouragement, and, above all, for her loving companionship.

Madeline Gilmore, for organizing, editing, and formatting the book into some coherence.

For Gloria Loomis and Julia Masnik, my stalwart agents and guardian angels.

With much affection for Bradford Morrow, who gave several of these stories a home.

For Erika Goldman, lover of literature, who takes chances.

Previous Publication History and Prizes

These stories appeared previously in the publications listed below.

"Winter, 1965": *BOMB*, Fall 2014; *Pushcart Prize XL: Best of the Small Presses*, ed. Bill Henderson, 2016. Winner of the Pushcart Prize 2016 and the O. Henry Prize 2016.

"The Veranda": In "Shadow Selves," ed. Bradford Morrow, *Conjunctions* 54 (Spring 2010). Winner of the Pushcart Prize 2012.

"The Snow on Tompkins Square Park": In "A Menagerie," ed. Bradford Morrow, *Conjunctions* 61 (Fall 2013).

"The Bar at Twilight": In "Nocturnals," ed. Bradford Morrow, *Conjunctions* 72 (Spring 2019).

"The Tower": In "In Absentia," ed. Bradford Morrow, *Conjunctions* 60 (Spring 2013). Winner of the Pushcart Prize 2015.

"In the Borghese Gardens": *The New Review of Literature* 1 (October 2003).

"The Café, the Sea, Deauville, 1966": In "Inside Out: Architectures of Experience," ed. Bradford Morrow, *Conjunctions* 68 (Spring 2017).

"Lives of the Artists": *The Worlds of Joaquín Torres-García*, exhibition catalogue, Acquavella Galleries, New York (New York: Rizzoli, 2018).

"Allegory: A Parable": *Allegory*, exhibition catalogue, Joseph Helman Gallery, New York, 1997.

"The Phantom Tower": In *The Photographic Work of Robin Broadbent* (Bologna, Italy: Damiani, 2017).

"Delacroix in Love": *EAST*, August 2016.

"Nine Flowers": Originally appeared as "Nine Flowers in Three Sanctuaries" in "Sanctuary: The Preservation Issue," ed. Bradford Morrow, *Conjunctions* 70 (Spring 2018). Reprinted as "Nine Flowers" in artist's book with screen print by Ross Bleckner, Planthouse Gallery, New York, 2019.

"The Garden Party": *Martin Mull: Endgame*, exhibition catalogue, Hirschl & Adler Galleries, New York, February 2015. Reprinted in *The Los Angeles Review of Books*, August 2015.

"The Restaurant. The Concert. The Bar. The Bed. *Le Petit Déjeuner*": *BOMB*, Spring 2022.

"L'Odyssée": *Jeff Koons: Popeye Series*, exhibition catalogue, Serpentine Gallery, London (Köhn: Walther König, 2009).

"Some Episodes in the History of My Reading": In "Speaking Volumes," ed. Bradford Morrow, *Conjunctions* 63 (Fall 2014). Notable Mention, *The Best American Essays 2015*, ed. Ariel Levy.

About the Author

Frederic Tuten grew up in the Bronx. At age fifteen, he dropped out of high school to become a painter and live in Paris, but that youthful dream went unrealized. He took odd jobs and studied briefly at the Arts Students League, and eventually went back to school, continuing on to earn a Ph.D. in early-nineteenth-century American literature from New York University.

He later traveled through Latin America, studying pre-Columbian art and Mexican mural painting at Universidad Nacional Autónoma de México (UNAM), wrote about Brazilian Cinema Novo, and joined that circle of filmmakers, which included Glauber Rocha and Nelson Pereira dos Santos. Tuten finally did live in Paris, where he taught film and literature at the University of Paris 8. He acted in a short film by Alain Resnais, cowrote with the director Andrzej Żuławski the cult film *Possession*, and conducted summer writing workshops with Paul Bowles in Tangier.

Tuten has written essays and fiction for artists' catalogues, including those of John Baldessari, Eric Fischl,

Pierre Huyghe, Jeff Koons, Mona Kuhn, David Salle, Ross Bleckner, and Roy Lichtenstein.

He has published five novels: *The Adventures of Mao on the Long March*; *Tallien: A Brief Romance*; *Tintin in the New World*; *Van Gogh's Bad Café*; and *The Green Hour*. He has also published two books of short stories, *Self-Portraits: Fictions* and *The Bar at Twilight*, and a memoir, *My Young Life*.

Tuten received a Guggenheim Fellowship for fiction and the Award for Distinguished Writing from the American Academy of Arts and Letters. He lives in New York.

Bellevue Literary Press is devoted to publishing literary fiction and nonfiction at the intersection of the arts and sciences because we believe that science and the humanities are natural companions for understanding the human experience. We feature exceptional literature that explores the nature of perception and the underpinnings of the social contract. With each book we publish, our goal is to foster a rich, interdisciplinary dialogue that will forge new tools for thinking and engaging with the world.

To support our press and its mission,
and for our full catalogue of published titles,
please visit us at blpress.org.

Bellevue Literary Press
New York